Rekindling the Widower's Heart

Glynna Kaye

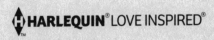

HARLEQUIN® LOVE INSPIRED®

Recycling programs
for this product may
not exist in your area.

 LOVE INSPIRED BOOKS

ISBN-13: 978-0-373-81867-9

Rekindling the Widower's Heart

www.Harlequin.com

Printed in U.S.A.

"She looks like a princess in a book, doesn't she, Daddy?"

He glanced at Delaney, studying her, almost as if seeing her for the first time.

He abruptly looked away. "Yes, she does, Chloe."

Luke shifted the child in his arms and she looped her own around his neck to settle in once more. Her eyes were growing heavier by the minute.

"Say good-night to Delaney."

The girl waved. "Good night, Delaney."

Luke nodded in Delaney's direction, as well.

"Why don't you lock up and I'll see you to your car?"

"Thanks, but I'll be fine. It's not even completely dark yet."

"It will be shortly. Chloe and I will see you there, then follow you to your place. Make sure you get inside safely."

From the look in his eyes, there would be no point in debating the issue.

"Okay. Thanks." She returned to the kitchen to secure the dead bolt at the back door. She suddenly felt like Chloe must feel when cradled in her father's strong arms. Safe. Protected.

It was nice to know someone cared.

Glynna Kaye treasures memories of growing up in small Midwestern towns—and vacations spent with the Texan side of the family. She traces her love of storytelling to the times a houseful of great-aunts and great-uncles gathered with her grandma to share candid, heartwarming, poignant and often humorous tales of their youth and young adulthood. Glynna now lives in Arizona, where she enjoys gardening, photography and the great outdoors.

Trust in the Lord with all your heart and lean not on your own understanding. In all your ways submit to Him and He will make your paths straight.
—*Proverbs* 3:5–6

Be strong and courageous. Do not be afraid; do not be discouraged, for the Lord your God will be with you wherever you go.
—*Joshua* 1:9

To my editor, Melissa Endlich.

Thank you for partnering with me
to share my stories with the readers of Love Inspired.
This is truly a dream come true!

Chapter One

"Not everyone is meant to be in your life forever, I guess."

Taken aback by the unexpected, too-close-to-home observation, Luke Hunter placed a work-booted foot on the bottom step of the empty storefront's covered concrete porch, doing his best not to frown at the attractive blonde perched on the railing.

"But that's why," she concluded with a dazzling smile that made his breath catch, "we need to make the most of every moment, don't you think? Enjoy life to the full with a thankful heart. That's what's bringing me to Hunter Ridge—mountain country Arizona—for the summer."

Until her red Ford Focus had pulled up in front of the rental property fifteen minutes late, a Beach Boys tune belting out of the stereo and her long, sun-streaked hair tumbling around her shoulders, he'd never before laid eyes on Delaney Marks. Although attempting to listen closely, he didn't quite grasp the entirety of the convoluted tale of what brought her into his world that afternoon. But, as near as he could piece together, it had something to do with the departure of a boyfriend, an aunt in poor health, and following her heart.

"Then I hope—" he managed something he trusted was akin to a smile "—that this property is what you're looking for."

"Oh, it is." She turned to gaze down the ponderosa pine-lined road that curved through the little town's business district, then back at him. "I looked at it online before I made this appointment. It's ideal."

Why were all these artsy types continuing to flock here anyway? Why not Sedona? Jerome? Someplace where they'd fit in and wouldn't annoy the locals.

Without a doubt, this young woman fit the stereotype, with denim-look leggings, an embroidered turquoise tunic and dainty leather sandals. Silver hoop earrings glinted when she tilted her head, and a bracelet shimmered around her ankle. Was there a finger on either hand not encircled with a ring?

Yesterday, the second day of June, Grandma Jo—Josephine Davis Hunter—told the extended family that a woman had called about renting a property along Hunter Ridge Road. No doubt another outsider determined to further change the character of their town.

Unfortunately, he'd drawn the short straw and had to deal with her today when he'd much rather be balancing the Hunter Enterprise books or—better yet—solidifying long overdue relocation plans. It was more than time he took his future into his own hands—despite what family members thought. Opportunity had knocked in the form of a potential job offer from two ex-army buddies in Kansas. He had only to wait for the door to swing open. Or give it a push.

"I assume, Ms. Marks," he said, "that you want to take a look inside?"

"I'd *love* to."

Her too-appealing mouth widened as she caught his eye with a startlingly flirtatious glance. An uncomfortable warmth crept up his neck. This wasn't the first time she'd openly looked at him that way, as if fancying what she saw.

Yeah, right. Like he was buying that.

Who could blame him for suspecting her motives? He was at least a decade older than her own fresh-faced mid-twenties. A military vet. A widower for the past six years. The single father of three. Barely keeping it all together. Even though she couldn't have known any of that when she breezed into town, he held no illusions that he came even close to what some pretty young babe was dreaming of.

But an hourglass figure and eyes sparkling with admiration wouldn't gain her a hoped-for advantage in any rental contract negotiations. He had a houseful of hungry mouths to feed and every dime counted.

Her gaze still holding his, she hopped off the railing to stand before him, close enough that he could see the sprinkling of freckles across her nose.

"And please, call me Delaney."

With a brisk nod, he unlocked the door of the two-story natural stone building. Nestled between a pottery shop and Hunter Ridge's version of a deli, the first floor housed an open space ideal for commercial use, with a studio apartment above. He motioned for her to precede him inside and caught her fresh, citrusy fragrance as she glided by.

Midafternoon sunlight slanted in from the open door and unshuttered windows, filling the high-ceilinged, wooden-floored space with an inviting glow. A faint scent of cinnamon lingered in the air, no doubt the persuasive touch of his aunt Jessi.

Spreading her arms wide as if embracing the interior, Ms. Marks—Delaney—gave a soft cry of delight that echoed through the spacious room. "I knew I'd love it."

"You understand, don't you," he said, feeling obligated to offer caution, "that leasing for three months rather than for an entire year means a higher monthly rental rate?" It was during the summer when Hunter Ridge—and the high elevation mountain country at large—made up for the economically slower months.

She shrugged. "No worries. I'm originally from Canyon Springs, so I totally get it."

Canyon Springs? That wasn't much over thirty minutes away, so why—

"I could hardly believe it," she continued, "when I saw this place on the property rental website. I'd been afraid I'd get stuck in an ugly, generic apartment complex."

"I don't think Hunter Ridge has too many of those."

She laughed and his heart beat faster at the sound of it, as refreshing as a cool drink of water on a hot day.

"No, probably not." She looked happily around her. "Your town has done an admirable job of retaining its rustic character, its backcountry ambience."

"We do our best to safeguard our heritage." Unfortunately, not as well as they should have in recent years.

Delaney strolled across the space, empty except for a massive iron woodstove on the far side of the main room. Then she spun toward him. "I can't believe this place hasn't already been snatched up. Is there something you're not telling me? Like the roof leaks or there's no indoor plumbing?"

He held up his hands in a gesture of innocence. "A couple from Flagstaff signed a lease, but unforeseen circumstances dictated that they break their contract a few days ago."

She closed her eyes momentarily and drew in a slow breath, almost as if communing with an unseen person. God? Then with a contented sigh she took a confident step toward him. "Meet your new tenant."

Had he heard right? "You haven't even seen all of it yet."

She didn't so much as slant him a sheepish look to indicate she recognized the impulsiveness of her decision. Clearly, she wasn't a stranger to spur-of-the-moment leaps.

"There's an apartment, too, right?"

"A studio in the loft." He motioned upward to a low wall that concealed a portion of the raftered space above. "Full bath. Kitchenette. There's a balcony overlooking a patio and toward the wooded properties farther up the ridge."

"I guess I should take a peek, huh?"

"Please do."

He couldn't help but notice how gracefully she crossed the room to the rear of the building, her gently waving hair flowing down the back of her petite frame. Just beyond the staircase she paused to look in an open door. "A half bath, too? Perfect."

"And a kitchen in the back."

She hadn't yet mentioned her intentions for the space, but Hunter Ridge would likely be welcoming another handmade candle shop or stained-glass studio for the summer season. Not exactly what the town needed. At least, however, the town council—one member of which he had the privilege of calling Mom—might sleep better at night with another source of income added to the roster.

He watched with more interest than he was willing to admit as Delaney poked her head into the kitchen, then peeped out the back door window before returning to the main room and heading up to the loft, her footsteps sounding lightly on the wooden stairs.

The next thing he knew, she peered down at him from over the low wall, dimples bracketing a wide smile. "Just as I thought. Love at first sight. Where do I sign?"

No haggling? No pointing out that he'd already laid claim to the previous person's forfeited deposit so he could afford to cut her a sweeter deal? But in this economy, he wasn't about to look a gift horse in the mouth.

"Come on down, then, and we'll do business."

While few Hunter Ridge natives cared for the influx of newcomers, the bottom line could be a hard taskmaster. But the interlopers would pay well to snag a piece of this mountain country paradise. For that very reason, Delaney's showstopping smile would serve to little advantage. While the engaging look she occasionally cast his way sparked an almost forgotten flicker of masculine satisfaction, he tamped it down. He had neither the time nor the energy for flirtatious females.

Been there, done that.

And, God help him, he was still paying the price.

Less than an hour later, Luke Hunter rose from behind a wooden desk to drop two keys into Delaney's outstretched palm.

"Welcome to Hunter Ridge."

"Thank you." But despite his hospitable-sounding words, it was clear the sober-eyed Luke Hunter wasn't thrilled at the prospect of renting the place to her. Not that he was hostile, exactly. Maybe *resigned* was a more accurate word.

In a town with too many empty storefronts, you'd think he'd have laid on a thick coat of persuasion to prevent her from marching down the street to the next available space. Instead, when they'd retreated to the offices of Hunter Enterprises, across the blacktop road and a few doors down from what was to be her new summer abode, he'd practically tried to talk her out of signing. But parking limitations, minuscule dimensions of the apartment, and precautions regarding the woodstove didn't faze her in the least.

This summer was to be a chance not only to help the local church youth ministry while remaining conveniently close to her aunt in Canyon Springs, but an opportunity to find out if her artistic talents held any merit. Would her skills eventually rescue her from a lifetime with her nose pressed to a computer monitor?

"I can hardly wait to move in." She stood, tucking the keys and paperwork into her over-size woven purse, a tingle of anticipation skimming up her spine. But whether that was solely rooted in God leading her to an ideal property for the summer or founded in the somewhat hesitant smile her handsome new landlord had just bestowed, she couldn't be sure.

Probably a bit of both.

She rewarded his effort with a high-wattage smile of her own, but he frowned ever so slightly and abruptly stepped to a shelving unit to purposefully peruse its contents.

Was he shy? Unsociable? Or a man with more important things on his mind than the eagerness of a new tenant embarking on a summer adventure?

Nevertheless, she again couldn't help but notice how he held himself with an almost military bearing, the overhead light that illuminated his neatly clipped, sandy brown hair also emphasizing the strong planes of his face. No, he didn't appear to be a man who'd empathize with her bubbling enthusiasm, nor had she missed the flicker of censure in his eyes when she'd presented her photo ID. He'd clearly been unimpressed by the evidence of her recent California residency.

Finding what he was looking for, Luke pulled a navy blue folder from a shelf and handed it to her. "Hunter Ridge Chamber of Commerce" it proclaimed in raised lettering. The possible significance of his last name and that of the community hadn't been lost on her.

"Although you can find this information online, I keep a few of these on hand." He motioned to the folder as she flipped through its contents. "Since water, gas and electricity are included, you won't need to make those arrangements. You mentioned, too, that opening a business isn't your intent, so those sections won't pertain to you, either."

"The space will be my studio." Loving the sound of that—so artistic and professional—she proudly held out both hands, palms downward, to display her rings. "I make jewelry and hope to sell it through the Hunter Ridge Artists' Cooperative."

The corners of Luke's mouth dipped downward, but he made no comment. Instead, he briefly studied the varied ring designs, then gave a brisk nod. "Very nice."

"Thanks." She slowly drew back her hands, irritated with herself for hoping to hear something more along the lines of a few oohs and aahs. When had she become so insecure, constantly in need of reassurance regarding her craft?

A telltale muscle tightened in her throat. Since both Aunt Jen and Dwayne Moorley dismissed her artistic efforts as having no significance, that's when.

She drew in a reviving breath. "I've been making jewelry for myself and friends since a high school art class introduced me to working with silver. But it's time to see what the rest of the world thinks."

"I wish you the best, then."

Would it be too much to hope that friends and family members would feel the same? If she turned her back on the education her aunt had sacrificed to provide for a pretty much penniless, parentless niece, there would be few who wouldn't think her a foolish and most ungrateful young woman. She no longer cared about Dwayne's opinion, but would Aunt Jen ever forgive her?

With that sobering thought, she nevertheless managed a cheery farewell, and spun toward the door, away from Luke Hunter's probing gaze.

"Oh!"

Tottering dangerously, her attempt at a poised exit faltered as the dog she'd tripped over leaped aside with a pitiful yelp.

Luke caught her by the upper arm with a steadying grip. "Are you okay?"

Warmth crept into her cheeks as she stared for a too-long moment into his intense blue eyes, her heart beating at an erratic clip. Then, with a self-conscious laugh, she slipped free of his grasp and stepped away, once again secure on her own two feet. "I'm fine, so you can relax. I'm not the suing type."

He looked momentarily taken aback. Then glanced down at the German shepherd that had retreated behind his master. "It's fortunate, then, that Rags isn't, either."

Shouldn't that quip have been accompanied by a smile? But she didn't spy so much as a trace of a grin on his face.

Nevertheless, she knelt down to call softly to the dog and, after only a moment's hesitation, he trotted to her, tail wagging, to be petted. "Sorry, big guy."

Amends made, she rose to her feet once more, only to be caught off-guard by an unexpected sadness in Luke's eyes. She'd stepped on his dog, tossed out ill-received lawsuit humor and made peace with the pup. Surely none of those things had wounded his feelings.

But he didn't look inclined to share his thoughts, so she bid him a hasty adieu and departed.

Once outside, she paused to catch her breath and take in the hodgepodge of older stone and frame buildings along the tree-lined road. Some snuggled against each other as if for mutual support, others were stand-alones with towering ponderosas pressing in close. A few, obviously vacant, stared almost forlornly at their more fortunate, occupied neighbors. But despite evidence to the contrary, Delaney sensed the promise of renewed life in the community.

A life she hoped to tap into this summer.

Her heart lightening, she angled across the road to her new home, then trotted up the steps. The summer held so much potential, a freedom she hadn't experienced since college graduation. And who was to say she couldn't arrange to bump into Luke Hunter more frequently than anticipated? After all, this was a small town.

And he did have amazing blue eyes.

No wedding ring, either.

She snatched up a flier tucked into the edge of the door, then inserted the key in the dead-bolt lock. If she could somehow banish that cheerless look she'd glimpsed and coax out a few smiles, the summer might be especially fun.

But she'd barely gripped the doorknob when a shadow emerged from the corner of her mind, halting her flight of fancy. With a sigh, she pushed open the door and stepped inside. Would she never learn? As Aunt Jen often reminded, when something—or someone—looked too good to be true, it usually was.

Standing in the shadows, Luke held aside the office curtain and gazed toward the property Delaney Marks would be occupying for the next three months. She'd unlocked the door, briefly disappeared inside, and was now pulling a suitcase out of the backseat of her car.

"You're not going to believe this, big guy," he said to the dog seated at his feet. "She's moving in already."

Big guy. That's what his wife had called Rags from the time he was a tiny puppy. Odd that Delaney called him that, too, though he wasn't the largest of his breed.

Luke's gaze lingered as the new tenant tucked a floral sleeping bag under her arm and dragged an oversize pink suitcase up the porch steps. Talk about an optimist. She was eager to stretch her wings. To reach for her dreams. To taste all life had to offer.

He'd been like that once. A long time ago.

But watching her now, bubbling with energy and excitement, made him feel…old.

With an almost cheerful announcement that she was currently unemployed due to a layoff, she nevertheless hadn't flinched when writing a substantial check. And when he'd requested ID, she'd handed him a Golden State driver's license that confirmed his suspicions—she'd be only twenty-seven come August. But her birthdate also served as a reminder that nineteen years ago when he'd left Hunter Ridge, thinking that at age eighteen he was rough and tough and all grown up, she'd barely reached the tender age of eight years old.

Practically a baby.

Yeah, she was a pretty, vivacious little thing and it had been a long time since a woman had caught his eye. But he was an old codger in comparison. A father of two teens and an eight-year-old, a man weighed down with responsibilities that a young woman would want no part of.

"She's as close to my son's age as she is to mine," he said aloud with a shake of his head.

The dog bumped against his leg as if in sympathy, and Luke noticed Delaney had returned to the car to haul out a box from the passenger-side front seat.

"I should go over to help her unload, don't you think?" he said to Rags. "That would be the neighborly thing to do."

But before he could turn away from the window, a white minivan with a Christ's Church of Hunter Ridge logo pulled up next to her car. One of Luke's cousins—a younger *bachelor* cousin— hopped out of the driver's side with a welcoming smile.

Garrett, who already had to beat women off with a stick.

"Just as well." Luke tugged the curtain back into place. Despite the not-so-subtle signals that she wouldn't be opposed to getting to know him better, he'd steer clear of Delaney Marks.

He drew in a heavy breath as a too-familiar

weight settled in his chest. No cradle robbing for him.

Besides, what kind of woman would take to a man who'd as good as wished his wife dead?

Chapter Two

"Let's get Luke over here and see if he can figure this out." Pastor Garrett McCrae gave the microwave's buttons one last pointless push. Then, with an it-beats-me shake of his head, he stepped back. "There's a trick to it and he'll likely know it."

Delaney looked up from where she was seated on the ceramic-tiled floor beside an open cardboard box, searching for another mug and a wider variety of teas.

"I hate to bother him." While she didn't mind seeing Luke again—only thirty minutes after they'd parted—she didn't want her new landlord to think she'd be a problem tenant.

"No biggie." Garrett pulled out his cell phone and punched in a speed dial number. "That's why God created cousins. For bothering."

"You and Luke are cousins?"

He nodded as he held the phone to his ear. "His dad is my mom's brother."

Delaney mentally logged that enlightening bit of information as she studied him, looking for a family resemblance. Maybe in the eyes, though

Garrett's were more gray than blue and accented with laugh lines. His hair was darker as well. Older than her but younger than Luke, Garrett and his cousin hadn't come from the same mold.

When the call was picked up on the other end, Garrett immediately launched in. "Hey, cuz. I'm helping our summer youth volunteer get moved in to Charlie and Emma's old place and— What? Yeah, right. You let that slip by you?" Garrett chuckled. "You'll appreciate that she'll be keeping teens with too much time on their hands out of trouble. Anyway, the microwave downstairs isn't working."

Delaney watched as Garrett paused to listen intently, then he gave her a thumbs-up before pocketing his phone. "He's on his way."

Anticipation mingled with apprehension. "I hope he doesn't think I'm going to be a nuisance."

Garrett shrugged. "Being pestered is good for him. Gets him out of his comfort zone."

Having moved back to the main room to wait for Luke, the door standing open to admit the scent of sun-warmed pine, they again marveled at their providential good fortune. Only last Sunday evening Garrett had been in contact with her aunt's pastor in Canyon Springs—who happened to know of Delaney's availability for a summer position.

"I can hardly believe the perfect timing," Delaney concluded. "With Aunt Jen's health in question, I needed an excuse to stick relatively close by this summer."

"Believe me, we're more than happy to have you here."

"I'm glad. And thanks for helping me carry in my stuff."

Garrett glanced at the suitcase, sleeping bag and boxes by the door. "This isn't everything you have, is it?"

"It's all I could cram in my car to bring over this afternoon. The apartment in Sacramento was furnished, so I'll be borrowing furniture from my aunt and friends in Canyon Springs. I do have a few more boxes, clothes and my bicycle."

"I'm sure folks here at the church will be happy to loan you whatever else you may need. As I'd mentioned earlier, with our youth intern forced to pull out at the last minute, you'll be considered an answered prayer."

"Maybe, maybe not," said the low, mellow voice of the pastor's cousin, carrying from the open door. "Better plan on a few disgruntled looks when Delaney is introduced on Sunday rather than David."

She turned to Luke with a laugh, trusting his comment was teasing, even though his tone didn't reflect that. "I hope no one is *too* disappointed."

He shrugged, unsmiling. "You never know."

Okay, maybe he wasn't teasing.

"Disappointed?" Garrett shot his cousin an aggravated look. "Not a chance."

"I'm giving her fair warning." Luke leaned a broad shoulder against the doorjamb and crossed his arms. "Last Sunday you were singing the praises of that college kid, claiming he'd be a big draw for the local teens with his background in biblical studies and enthusiasm for outdoor sports. You got the boys fired up that he was big into hiking and mountain biking."

Luke cut an apologetic glance at Delaney as if to acknowledge it was no fault of hers that her only claim to fame was making jewelry. Then his eyes narrowed in speculation as he directed a pointed look at his cousin.

Garrett merely offered a serene smile. "God moves in mysterious ways."

"Right." Luke pushed away from the door. "Now let's take a look at that microwave problem."

He strode to the back of the building, Delaney almost scampering behind him, eager to explain why his afternoon had been interrupted.

"Pastor McCrae—I mean, Garrett—attempted to warm a mug of peppermint tea, but—"

"Peppermint tea?" With a glance in Garrett's direction, Luke raised disbelieving brows.

The pastor only shrugged, his impish smile unapologetic.

"Anyway," Delaney continued, wanting Luke

to get the full story, "when he put the mug in the microwave and pressed the start button, nothing happened."

"Zip," Garrett confirmed. "I told Delaney there's probably a trick to it. A secret knock or something."

Luke took a slow breath, his tone dry. "There's a trick to it all right."

Garrett cast Delaney an I-told-you-so look.

Squatting in front of the wooden microwave cart, Luke reached underneath. Then he pulled out a length of electrical cord, waved the plug end at his cousin and poked it in the wall outlet.

"Well, what do you know?" Garrett laughed, not the least bit embarrassed.

But she was. Heat scorched her cheeks. Luke probably thought her a total airhead. Why hadn't she taken a look herself before Garrett called him? "I'm sorry. It didn't even dawn on me that it might not be plugged in."

Luke looked down at her, a faint light of amusement in his eyes. "No problem. It's my fault. I forgot Uncle Mac would have unplugged everything when the tenant vacated last fall. A safety precaution. Usually new renters don't move in fifteen minutes after they sign the lease, so there'd normally be time to get everything hooked up and the refrigerator cooling."

He ran his hand roughly through his hair in an almost weary gesture—again confirming he had more important things on his mind. "Give me a few minutes and I'll plug in the rest of the appliances down here and in the loft."

Garrett playfully punched him in the shoulder. "This is something you couldn't have told me over the phone, cuz?"

Luke drew back. "Are you kidding? And miss an opportunity to publicly demonstrate the shortcomings of our good pastor?"

"He lives for that," Garrett acknowledged with a smile in Delaney's direction. "But all's well that ends well, right?"

Luke moved past her to the refrigerator, his height seeming even more imposing in the confined space.

"Hey, while you're in a Boy Scout frame of mind…" Garrett stepped in to assist in pulling the large appliance away from the wall. "Delaney has furniture and more boxes to bring over from Canyon Springs. Do you think you and that big pickup of yours could help her out?"

Luke glanced up from where he'd plugged in the fridge, then slowly rose to his feet. "Now?"

"No, not now," Delaney quickly inserted, catching the reluctance in his tone. "Besides, I can always recruit someone from Canyon Springs."

Garrett helped push the now-humming refrigerator back into place. "Luke can do it. When would work best for you, Delaney?"

"Today's Thursday. So tomorrow, maybe? Or

Saturday? Before Sunday evening, if possible." But she wasn't convinced that her new landlord was buying into the volunteer gig. "The youth group can always sit on the floor, but it will be more relaxing with a few comfy chairs and a sofa. I'd rather not resort to folding chairs. They're too stiff and formal."

Kids didn't much care for being rowed up or in a too-rigid circle. As she remembered from her own youth group days and as a high school youth leader when in college, a casual setting would be more conducive to building relationships and drawing out participation.

Garrett's eyes brightened. "Awesome idea. This place is perfect."

"You want the kids to meet *here*?" Luke's disapproval of her plan was clearly evident. "What's wrong with the fellowship hall where they usually meet?"

Garrett gave his cousin an incredulous look. "The remodel, remember? It starts Monday and the place will be torn up for weeks. This is much better than resorting to a Sunday school classroom."

"But—"

Garrett turned to Delaney, cutting Luke off. "I don't have any objections. This place is spacious and centrally located. The kids will love it. I'll get the word out."

Luke pinned Garrett with a doubtful look.

"Don't you think you should run it by the church board first?"

"Mmm…" Garrett narrowed his eyes as if in deep thought, then shook his head. "No."

An unsmiling Luke wagged a finger at him. "One of these days, buddy, you're going to overstep your bounds as an interim pastor and find yourself shown the door."

Interim pastor? He wasn't the real deal? Had he overstepped his bounds by bringing her on board two days ago?

Unfazed, Garrett grinned as he pulled out his cell phone and read an incoming text message. "You'd be leading the lynch mob, I assume?"

"Guarantee it."

Garrett held up his phone. "Hey, looks like I'm late for a meeting. I'll leave you two here to work out details for the move. Think you can handle that, Luke, without causing too much trauma to your schedule?"

"I can handle it." Luke gave Garrett a steady look as he walked him to the door, Delaney trailing along behind.

The pup was getting way too big for his britches these days and, as usual, he was doing his best to push his older cousin's buttons. To Luke's irritation, Garrett maintained, as did the rest of the extended family, that he spent too much time working at Hunter Ridge Enterprises. And seeing to the never-ending needs of his kids.

Like it was any of their business. Little did they know that if all went well, he'd soon be out from under their scrutiny.

But why was Garrett fobbing off the youth volunteer on him? The way he was all smiles and bending over backwards to accommodate her this afternoon—*peppermint tea?*—it appeared he intended to keep her to himself. Then again, maybe the interim pastor of Christ's Church didn't see him as competition for the much younger lady's attention. It reminded him of a situation when, as a kid, Garrett had left a favored toy in the protective custody of their aged grandpa.

With a wave of his hand, Garrett headed out the door. "I'll take a rain check on that tea, Delaney. But stop by my office tomorrow morning and we'll get the paperwork completed."

As soon as he'd departed, she spun toward Luke, her expression uncertain. "Please don't feel obligated to help me move because your cousin is…pushy."

She thought Garrett was pushy? Perceptive. "I don't mind. It's just—"

"That you're a big boy and prefer making your own decisions?" Mischief lit her eyes and, in response, he felt the tug of his own somewhat rusty smile.

"I've done that for quite a few years."

For ten more than she had.

"It's bad enough that you had to come over here to plug in a microwave." For a moment she covered her face with her hands, her expressive eyes peeping at him from between ringed fingers. "How embarrassing."

"Don't be embarrassed. Like I said, it's my fault. And if I hadn't wanted to rib Garrett in person, I could have enlightened him over the phone." But if he'd told him over the phone, he wouldn't be standing here right now talking to their pretty new tenant. Had that possibility played a part in his decision to see to the microwave in person?

Naw. He'd wanted only to give his cousin a hard time. He'd take care of business here and be on his way. Chloe, his youngest, would be arriving any time now and expect him to be at the office after school on a Thursday afternoon.

He gave Delaney a reassuring nod. "I'll take care of the appliances upstairs and make sure things are in order with the hot water heater and the furnace. It gets chilly around here some nights."

"I've always loved that about Arizona mountain country." She opened her arms wide as if to encompass the world around her, a spontaneous gesture he'd observed earlier when she'd claimed the rental property as her own. "You regulate how cool you want to be by how wide you open a window."

"You said you were originally from Canyon Springs?"

She shrugged. "I moved there when I was fourteen."

Something flickered through her eyes and he sensed a story untold. But he wouldn't press her for details. The less he knew about their new tenant's personal life, the better off he'd be. Although…if she'd be hanging out with Anna and Travis and the youth group this summer, it might be worthwhile to get to know her better. A parent had to be proactive these days when it came to who you allowed to influence your kids. Delaney was awfully young to be taking on responsibility for the group.

He cleared his throat. "So, how would tomorrow afternoon work for you to retrieve the rest of your belongings?"

She tilted her head. "You're sure?"

"I'm good with it. After lunch? I could pick you up at one o'clock." If Garrett couldn't tag along to help with the sofa, he'd get one of his friends in the neighboring town to assist, then recruit another family member back here to unload.

"I'll be ready. And thanks."

"No problem. But I guess I'd better finish up and get on out of here so you can get settled in." He turned away, intending to head to the loft, then tensed as he glimpsed a colorful flier atop Delaney's luggage by the door. He motioned toward it. "Where'd you get that?"

"What?" She turned to see what he was referring to. "Oh. I found that tucked in my door. Haven't even looked at it yet."

She picked it up. Flipped it over. "It looks as if someone plans to run for town council. There's a preliminary campaign gathering Monday night."

Someone intended to run for an opening on the town council all right. Sunshine Carston. An outspoken young woman who settled in town a couple of years ago and rallied a growing number of local artists to take a more active role in the community. She'd been a thorn in the side of quite a few longtime Hunter Ridge residents.

He slipped the flier from Delaney's fingers and glanced down at the photograph of the woman who would be his mother's probable opponent this coming fall. An attractive, eloquent young woman but, oh, what a pain in the neck at times.

"One word of advice, Delaney."

The blonde stared up at him with a slight frown. "And what would that be?"

"If you want the kind of summer you're hoping for, steer clear of local politics."

A dimple surfaced in her smooth cheek, the frown evaporating. "That bad, huh?"

"Could be." He returned the flier and she

folded it in half before tossing it back to the top
of the suitcase.

"I assure you that while I do my civic duty at
the polls, I've never been interested much in politics. However..." She flashed him a smile that
forced his heart rate up a notch. "Should you decide to run against Miss Sunshine there, I might
consider joining *your* team."

Warmth heated the back of his neck. Was she
only teasing? Flirting again? He was so out of
practice with that sort of stuff. Local ladies had
long ago given up the chase, which suited him
fine. He had no intention of sticking around
Hunter Ridge much longer anyway.

He took a step back. "Thanks for the vote of
support, but no politicking for me."

She didn't look surprised at his statement, only
amused. With effort, he drew his gaze from hers.

"Guess I'll get things checked out here and be
on my way."

But he'd barely started up the stairs to the loft
when a dog barked from the open door behind
him and a much-loved voice called out.

"We found you, Daddy!"

With a grin, he reached the bottom of the staircase before eight-year-old Chloe, raced forward
to launch herself into his arms for a welcoming
hug. He laughed as he scooped up the dark-haired
girl and she planted a kiss on his cheek. It was the
highlight of his day. "You've missed me?"

"Uh-huh. This much." With a giggle he never tired of hearing, her arms tightened around his neck and she gave him another kiss.

That's when he caught sight of Delaney standing off to the side, an uncertain look coloring her expression.

"Delaney? I want you to meet my daughter, Chloe." He didn't try to keep the pride out of his voice. "Chloe, this is Delaney Marks. She's going to be living in here this summer."

"Good to meet you, Chloe." Delaney reached out her hand and his little girl shyly shook it.

Then, a frown puckering her forehead, Chloe looked around the open space. "Why don't you have furniture?"

Delaney laughed, catching his eye. "I'll have furniture just as soon as your dad helps me move it in."

Chloe looked at him solemnly. "You'd better get busy, Daddy."

"I guess so. And I guess we'd better get going as soon as I check a few things out upstairs." He lowered his daughter to the floor and set her on her feet. "Homework tonight?"

She shook her head, not meeting his gaze.

Likely story. "Homework tonight?"

She started to shake her head again, then giggled and nodded, reaching out to clasp his hand in both of hers as she looked up at him mischievously.

"You don't need to check the appliances upstairs," Delaney said, drawing his attention again. "Despite recent evidence to the contrary, I'm perfectly capable of poking plugs into outlets."

He couldn't help but smile. "So you say."

"If I run into any unforeseen difficulties, I know where to find you, right?"

Her words sounded flirtatious enough, but had the interest he thought he'd recognized earlier diminished somewhat since the arrival of his child?

"That you do," he confirmed, irritated that he longed to ignite the spark in her gaze once again.

"Well, then?" She made a sweeping motion toward the door. "Be on your way."

Yes, on his way. And the farther he stayed from Delaney Marks the better.

Chapter Three

Daddy. The next morning when she crawled out of her sleeping bag in the loft, Delaney was still chiding herself for being surprised her new landlord was a parent. Luke was older than her and an attractive, seemingly nice man. It wouldn't be unexpected for him to have been in a serious relationship. To have a kid.

But the no ring thing had thrown her off.

Was he a widower? Divorced? Either could account for the apparent sadness she'd glimpsed earlier in his eyes—a look that evaporated with the arrival of Chloe.

Even now, chatting on the phone with her closest friend early Sunday evening while awaiting the arrival of the youth group, Delaney couldn't stop thinking about Luke Hunter. About how he'd scooped the squealing child into his arms with a smile that transformed his already handsome features. Brought him to life.

"Actually, I'm not too swamped with wedding preparations to keep me from popping over to see your new place." Paris Perslow's voice carried over the phone with a surprisingly carefree lilt for someone who was only weeks away from her wedding day. Most brides were a bundle of nerves at this point. "Like I said, we're keeping things simple, which is why you're my only attendant this time. Too bad Cody's best man is married."

"Believe me, that's for the best." Delaney's relationship with coworker Dwayne Moorley, like her job in Sacramento, had expired only weeks ago. This morning when drying her hair, she'd firmly reminded herself that although the outcome of their time spent together the past two years was disappointing, another unforeseen loss in her life, she wouldn't look back. In retrospect, she'd stayed in the relationship much too long, for reasons she was only now coming to fully understand.

"You're well rid of that guy," Paris continued as if reading her thoughts, ever loyal since a grieving Delaney, several years her junior, had arrived in Canyon Springs all those years ago. "He's way too controlling, thinking it's up to him to not only run his life, but yours, too. I'm beyond relieved you'll be my maid of honor without him showing up in my wedding photos."

"I, too, am delighted to save you from that blot on your special day." Delaney restlessly rose from the borrowed sofa to peep out a street-facing window where the sun cast lengthening shadows across the road. Movement caught her eye and hope sparked as she angled for a closer look. Was that activity in front of the Hunter Enterprises office? Yes. But, unfortunately, no one she knew. Only a handful of people who'd paused outside to visit.

She hadn't so much as caught a glimpse of Luke since he'd left with his daughter on Thursday. At their agreed-upon time Friday afternoon, two young men identifying themselves as cousins of Luke arrived with a pickup truck, offering an apology on his behalf.

How silly to be disappointed at the substitution. She was too old for crushes. Besides, even if Luke was a free agent, so to speak, an eight-year-old came with the package. So it was just as well.

"You *are* getting your jewelry into the Hunter Ridge Artists' Co-op, aren't you?"

Paris's words drew her back to the present. "It's not a sure thing. I have an appointment on Monday to present samples of my work. So say a prayer that they'll like what they see."

"They will. I absolutely love the earrings you made for me."

"I know Hunter Ridge's art community is small, not anything like Sedona, Jerome or Santa Fe, but if I can get my foot in the door here, it'll be a start. Hopefully, one that will encourage Aunt Jen to see my artistic leanings in a more positive light."

"I saw her at church this morning." Paris's words came cautiously. "I don't think she looks well."

"I don't think she does, either. But she insists

she's fine and is mad at me for taking the church position so I can stick around in case she needs me. She says the longer I'm unemployed, the more unemployable I'll become."

Which might well be true. But when her parents, widowed grandmother and younger sister had been killed in a car accident, her childless aunt and uncle had opened their home to her. Not too many years later, Uncle Del died in a boating accident, so how could she not be there for her aunt now?

"Well, I think you've made the right decision, Delaney. She's obviously not her usual self."

When the conversation ended with a reiteration of Paris's promise to visit soon, Delaney pocketed her cell phone and returned to the seating area. She had things remaining to be unpacked, but the open space now held a welcoming touch with soft lamplight and fat flickering candles rowed up on top of the woodstove. She'd arranged comfy, oversize throw pillows around the area for additional seating and, keeping the teenagers in mind, subs, chips and veggie sticks were on the coffee table.

Her introduction at the church service had gone well. Or at least she assumed so since no one had booed or thrown rotten eggs as Luke had led her to anticipate. But he and his daughter were nowhere to be seen that morning.

She straightened a stack of napkins, then stepped back to look around the room. She already loved this place, the openness of it and the way the sun shone through a fixed window at the front, above the porch. How the ponderosa pine branches cast moving shadows across the polished wooden floor.

Would the kids enjoy coming here?

And how would they respond to the annual summer project she'd chosen for them? With the help of Lois Grant, the women's ministry leader at the church, and a thumbs-up from Pastor McCrae, she'd quickly committed to an undertaking that was already near and dear to her heart. One that without a doubt had God's seal of approval, too.

"Delaney?"

With a sense of anticipation, she turned as the pastor of Christ's Church and a handful of teens stepped through the door. Introductions were quickly made. Brothers Kendrick and Nelson Bennett, both redheaded and freckle-faced, towered over her though they were probably not much older than sixteen. Curly-haired Sybil, her eyes rimmed in black as dark as her obviously colored tresses, wandered the room with interest, and "Scottie" Scott, a petite brunette with a pixie haircut, immediately made herself at home as well.

But Anna—a ponytailed, tomboyish-looking blonde dressed in well-worn Levi's, a striped knit top and Western boots—hung slightly back. Unlike the other teenage girls, her face was devoid of makeup but, nevertheless, a natural prettiness was clearly evident. Hunter, she'd said her last name was. Could half the town be somehow related?

Fifteen minutes later, when the group grew to a dozen teenagers chatting and meaningfully eyeing the food, Garrett clapped his hands to draw their attention.

"Let's give God thanks and dig in."

A murmur of agreement rippled among the young people and, following Garrett's prayer, they loaded their plates.

That's when she saw them in the doorway.

Without a doubt they were father and son, although the younger's darker hair, parted in the middle, lay in unruly layers down to his shoulders. As tall as his father standing beside him, the lankier, sullen-eyed teen brushed by the older man to saunter over to the seating area where he plopped down on the couch beside Scottie. Bare legs outstretched from his baggy, below-the-knee shorts and feet encased in leather sandals, he cast his father a you-can-leave-any-time-now stare. Then he deliberately slid his arm around the girl next to him and pulled her close.

Scottie giggled.

"Delaney." Luke leveled a meaningful look on the boy, who she guessed to be sixteen or seventeen. "I'd like you to meet my son, Travis."

The teen gave her a cursory nod of acknowledgment before reaching for a sandwich.

Luke frowned, then motioned to the pretty tomboy glaring at Travis. "I assume you've already met my daughter, Anna."

Delaney steadied herself with her hand to the back of a chair. Luke had three kids, not one? And two of them were *teenagers*?

The girl who'd earlier identified herself as a Hunter gave Delaney a reassuring smile, almost as if determined to make up for her older brother's dearth of manners. Delaney didn't see much resemblance between father and daughter. She must take after her mom.

Garrett made a sweeping motion toward the coffee table. "Help yourself to a sandwich, Luke. Delaney's put out quite a spread here."

Luke's querying gaze met hers as if seeking permission—and maybe forgiveness for his son's behavior?

She nodded encouragingly. "There's more than enough."

"Thanks." A barely-there smile surfaced, causing Delaney's heartbeat to skip. He looked especially attractive tonight in jeans and a blue T-shirt that not only matched his eyes but emphasized an unquestionably athletic frame. Thank goodness he'd eat and be on his way so she could keep her mind on the youth group business at hand.

Luke filled his plate, then settled on the floor between Nelson and Kendrick. But even after everyone had devoured most of the food, and Garrett's short devotion set the tone for an evening of Bible study, discussion and board games, Luke didn't seem in any hurry to depart.

To Delaney's surprise—and irritation—he didn't.

His son had outdone himself. He hadn't wanted to come, but Luke had insisted. Understandably, Travis was disappointed that the male college student slated for the summer had pulled out at the last minute. But there was no excuse for what he was doing tonight.

Delaney had graciously overlooked his behavior. But he could tell by her earlier almost nervous glances around the group as she'd tried unsuccessfully to encourage the sharing of personal experiences and spiritual challenges that his son's conduct had in many ways set the tone for the evening. He was a popular kid, one who the others looked up to. Despite the buoyant enthusiasm Delaney brought to the mix, if Travis decided youth group was no longer cool, well, it wasn't going to be cool to anybody else, either.

Then again, maybe Delaney wasn't a good fit. He glanced across the room where she'd returned from the kitchen with another supply of snacks. With Garrett called away, she was trying to get the attention of the now-laughing, chatting gathering of young folks setting up board games and paying her little attention.

A jolt of sympathy—and irritation—shot through him.

While Travis played a role in the evening's debacle, this was his cousin's fault. Garrett had allowed Delaney's bright smile and pretty face to sway his decision-making in selecting a replacement for the college intern. She was young and inexperienced and it was apparent that the kids, following Travis's lead, didn't view her as an adult leader.

But whoever's fault it was, he'd had enough of this.

His piercing whistle sliced through the high-ceilinged room, startling the kids into silence. They turned as one, eyes rounded, to his uncompromising glare. Then he gave a brisk nod toward the equally wide-eyed woman who was all but staring at him openmouthed, a flash of fire lighting her eyes.

She was mad at *him*?

"I think," he said, dismissing her reaction as he carefully looked at each young person present, "that Ms. Marks has something to say to you."

Cowed—except for Travis who cast him a disgruntled look—they all looked at her.

Standing before them, almost as if in front of a firing squad, she made an apologetic motion, the rings on her fingers catching the light.

"I... I won't interrupt your games long. I want to tell you a bit about the annual project the youth group will be doing this summer." A tentative smile touched her lips as she looked hopefully from face to face for signs of interest. But she avoided *his* gaze. "High Country Hope Ministries has the opportunity to move one of their disadvantaged families into larger accommodations, enabling a family that's been forced apart this past year to be reunited in a single dwelling."

"Cool," one boy chimed in, then popped a potato chip into his mouth.

"Yes, it is cool." Delaney's eyes now danced with excitement, the uncertainty replaced with an attractive glow. "And it's even cooler because we can help make that happen. The new property needs sprucing up—cleaning, interior painting, yard work and minor repairs."

Travis groaned and his girlfriend, Scottie, elbowed him.

Luke would be having a long talk with his son as soon as the opportunity presented itself.

"Their lease on the current property ends August thirty-first," Delaney continued, ignoring Travis, "but if we can help them make that move to the new place before the *first* of August, their current landlord—who has other plans for the property—will see that not only is Hope Ministries' deposit and August rent refunded, but they'll receive a bonus for vacating a month early."

"What will they do with the extra money?"

Leave it to Anna, his resident penny-pincher, to ask that kind of question.

"The refunded rent will go toward paying winter heating bills for the family and others. And the bonus…" Delaney looked around the circle of faces. "Will go to your youth group."

Kendrick sat up, suddenly interested. "We get the money?"

"For camp scholarships," Delaney was quick to clarify. "Or something along those lines to be decided by the church. But even more important than the money, our reward will be helping this family—father, mother and five children—live under one roof again."

"*Five* kids?" Travis leaned forward, pinning Delaney with a sharp look. "Don't tell me this house is for the Masons. That oldest kid of theirs is a real jerk. It was good riddance when he went to live with his loser dad last year."

Travis wasn't exaggerating. The same age as fifteen-year-old Anna, the Mason boy had been nothing but trouble. And "loser" wasn't an entirely inappropriate term for the kid's father, although Travis shouldn't have publicly called him that.

Lizzie Mason and her husband Benton were artsy types who'd settled here a few years ago. Working part-time jobs and selling their handcrafted wares, by their own choosing they'd not had an easy time of it and too often looked to others for assistance. Last summer Luke had an unpleasant run-in with Benton about delinquent rent on a commercial property and again the following autumn regarding Benton's son. Then came the drunk driving episode that resulted in injuries that put Benton out of work and into physical therapy and alcohol rehab.

Delaney had committed the youth group to a project helping people like that? Rewarding people who'd made no effort to take responsibility for their lives? Not a good idea.

Delaney hesitated now, as if unsure how to respond to Travis's question about the project family. "I believe…the name *is* Mason. The youngest is a twelve-year-old-girl."

A few kids groaned.

Travis flopped back on the sofa, arms folded. "*I'm* not helping any Masons."

A few kids laughed, but Scottie gave him a frosty look. "I think it's a good project. Samantha is a nice little girl. She can't help it that her father gets drunk."

"I agree," Sybil chimed in. "Cleaning and painting won't take that much of our time. We're supposed to help people in need, aren't we? And don't forget, the youth group gets the bonus money."

Several others nodded agreement.

But this project seemed destined for failure. Surely there were other worthy projects to pick from. Off the top of his head, he could think of several.

"We can talk about it further when I have more detailed information to share." Delaney gave Travis a look, as if expecting him to spout off again. "So I'll let you return to your activities now."

For a few silent minutes Delaney watched them settle back in to their board games, then headed to the kitchen. Grabbing the opportunity to speak with her in private, Luke joined her a few minutes later. When he rapped his knuckles on the door frame, she glanced up from the sink where she was rinsing dishes with a vengeance, then dried her hands on a dish towel, her eyes questioning.

Unexpectedly, his breath caught as the light glinted off the soft waves of golden hair. She'd pulled it off her forehead with a tiny green ceramic frog clip, and her peach-colored cotton top, adorned with embroidered butterflies, complemented her coloring and those beautiful hazel eyes.

"Is there something I can help you with, Luke? More snacks? Ice? Lemonade?"

"No, no. The food was great. Plentiful. Exactly what kids that age enjoy most."

She nodded as if relieved. "Good."

He leaned a shoulder against the refrigerator and studied her for a moment, not sure how to begin. "Actually, I want to apologize for Travis's behavior this evening."

Surprise flickered through her eyes.

"He's usually a laid-back kid, easy to get along

with. But something got into him tonight and we'll be having a talk when my temper cools."

She stared down at the floor for a moment, almost as if counting to ten, then back up at him. "Don't be too hard on him. You were right about what you'd mentioned the other day. Some of the kids, especially the boys, are disappointed that the original summer intern bailed."

"That's no excuse for discouraging the others from participating in this evening's planned activities. He basically shut down discussion."

She raised a delicate brow. "I'm not sure that it was entirely *Travis's* fault."

As he'd suspected, she was taking the blame. "Don't be too hard on yourself."

Her eyes widened. "I'm not—"

He held up his hand to stay the apology forming on her lips. "Tonight's behind us, tomorrow's a clean slate. But I do believe more thought needs to be given to your choice of summer projects."

A crease formed between her brows. "What do you mean?"

He shrugged. "You're new to town. You don't know the history behind the Masons. Benton's an artist whose last drunk driving episode got him thrown out of the house. Lizzie's trying to make a go of candle making and textile design, but why she insisted on staying here alone with four of the five children is beyond me. And now it sounds as if her husband and oldest son intend to come back to town, too. But Lizzie and Benton need to get their artsy heads out of the clouds, relocate and find real jobs."

"It's my understanding," Delaney said quietly, "that she's holding down several jobs and her husband has successfully completed alcohol rehabilitation."

"That's all well and good. But what if he comes back here and discovers nothing has changed? That making a go of their artistic pursuits is no more lucrative and parenting five kids isn't any easier now than it was before?"

Delaney again stared at the floor. That counting to ten business again. Then she raised her eyes to his. "I understand your concerns, but High Country Hope Ministries feels strongly that this family deserves a second chance. That they have a good possibility of succeeding this time. I've already committed us to it. We can't back out. They're counting on us."

With a shake of his head, he pushed away from the refrigerator. "What's the timeline on this again?"

"We have to be done by the end of July if Hope Ministries is to relocate the family, have the August rent returned and the youth group granted the bonus. Otherwise August thirty-first, with no refund and no bonus."

"That first deadline is only seven or eight weeks away." No, she hadn't thought this through.

"Kids have family vacations scheduled, music and sports camps, summer jobs. They aren't going to be available all day, every day. Maybe not much at all."

"I don't think it will take long to clean and paint. To do yard work. Garrett thought it entirely doable."

"You're assuming, too," he countered, "that you'll get buy-in from the kids. That Mason boy was a bully and a brat. Not well liked. Be prepared for pushback from some parents, too."

"Pushback?" She folded her arms, her chin lifting. "Like from you?"

"I'm not—" Well, maybe he was. "When will we get to take a look at this property?"

Her eyes narrowed—not caring for the *we* he'd thrown in there? He'd have found that fiery spark in her gaze more than a bit attractive had it not been leveled at him.

"I'm sorry, Delaney, but I'm not committing my kids to the project until I know more about it. Other parents will feel the same. Some of us have participated in past projects right along with our children. It's a good family bonding experience."

Her frown deepened. She took exception to fostering parent-kid time?

She took a deep breath. "I'll arrange for *us* to see the property this next week. Maybe invite parents for an overview meeting with a Hope

Ministries representative. Does that meet your expectations?"

"It's a start."

But it was clear that with Delaney in charge, he'd have to keep an even closer eye on the youth group. Exactly what he didn't have time for right now.

"Does Travis and Anna's dad come to a lot of the youth activities?"

Determined to calm—or confirm—her worst fears, Delaney had detained Garrett when he returned and everyone else dispersed for the night. It appeared she'd be seeing a lot of Mr. Hunter this summer, but under circumstances she'd prefer to avoid.

Garrett offered a grin. "He's one of those involved parents I mentioned to you earlier."

Involved.

As in engaged. Committed. On board.

In other words, in the way and messing up the youth group vibe.

How could she draw out the teens and get them to open up and share with her and each other if he conducted surveillance from the sidelines as he'd done this evening? When she'd hinted that tonight's less-than-satisfactory level of participation wasn't due solely to Travis, he'd had the gall to urge *her* not to blame herself.

And to think only a short while ago she'd

hoped to see him more often. Be careful what you wish for?

"Travis didn't seem too thrilled to have him here."

"When you were seventeen, would you have wanted your father keeping watch over you and your pals, listening in on every word you said?"

Actually, she'd have given almost anything if it meant her father would still be alive. But she could see there was a problem here. If her most recent encounter with Luke was indicative of what she could expect from him, he had an opinion on everything. And, like her ex-boyfriend and Aunt Jen, felt called upon to offer unsolicited advice.

"Have you talked to Luke about this?" Maybe she could enlist Garrett's support. "Explained that he needs to back off and give his teenagers breathing space?"

"Only a hundred times."

She placed her hands on her hips. Some people were clueless and it aggravated her that Luke was one of them. "Doesn't he realize being a helicopter dad, hovering over them all the time, isn't healthy for the kids—or for him?"

And it made *her* nervous.

"I think he's aware it causes friction at times, but it's hard for him to let go. He takes being a dad seriously."

Delaney snorted.

"Too seriously, if you ask me. Like, hello?" She

didn't care for Luke disrupting the youth group project dynamics. That is, if the project got off the ground. "I'm sure his kids think 'Get a life, Dad.'"

"Probably. But don't be too hard on him. He's had a rough time of it."

"How so?" Is this where she'd hear about the nightmare of an ex-wife? There had to be a story behind that sadness she sometimes glimpsed in his eyes, something beneath this overinvolved, overprotective dad stuff.

Garrett glanced away as if unwilling to say anything further.

"I assume," she prompted, not wanting to be left hanging, her questions unanswered, "you're alluding to a nasty divorce?"

For a long moment he remained silent. Then he shook his head.

"A divorce would be bad enough, but no. Not a divorce." He massaged the back of his neck with his hand, obviously reluctant to continue.

A knot formed in her stomach. Had the children's mother died as had hers? An accident? Health issues?

"If I'm going to spend my summer with these kids—and apparently their father, too—don't you think I should have a clear understanding of the situation?"

Garrett let out a pent-up breath. "Yeah, I suppose that's only fair. But if I tell you, you can't say anything to Luke, okay? He doesn't like to talk about it and he wouldn't like me or anyone else talking about it, either."

"I won't say anything." She mimed zipping her lips. "I promise."

"Then it's like this, Delaney…" Garrett's bleak gaze held hers. "Luke's wife—the mother of his kids—killed herself six years ago."

Chapter Four

Looking out the window where he was seated at the rustic Log Cabin Café, Luke paused, his coffee cup halfway to his lips.

Where was Delaney Marks off to this Monday morning, her head held high and a portfolio tucked under one arm? Her hair, swept into a low ponytail, bounced between her shoulder blades and a print skirt matching a solid sage-green top swirled around her ankles.

Oh, right. She'd said something about wanting to get her jewelry sold through the Hunter Ridge Artists' Co-op. Maybe that's where she was going? He didn't know a whole lot about that kind of thing, but he'd been honest when he'd said he liked her work. His younger sister Rio would likely pounce on one of those rings.

Now immediately across the road from the café, Delaney jerked to a halt. She started to turn away as if to return from where she'd come, then halted again. Opening the portfolio, she reached inside to check its contents. Then seemingly satisfied that all was as it should be, she closed it up and tucked it under her arm once again. And away she went.

He couldn't help but smile—and utter a silent prayer that she'd find a home for her jewelry. He wasn't particularly thrilled with the influx of artisans into town, but what could one more hurt?

"Enjoying the scenery, are you, Luke?"

Yanked from his reverie, he downed the remainder of his coffee and faced the café's owner. A big bruiser of a guy in his early sixties, he sported a shiny shaved head and close-cropped beard. A former Marine, he wasn't someone you'd care to meet in a dark alley if he didn't call you friend.

"Looks to be a nice day, Packy."

"I figured you might think that." His friend chuckled as Luke lifted a hand to stop a coffee refill. "Pretty gal, isn't she? I heard she's helping with the Christ's Church youth program this summer. Better keep an eye on Travis."

Packy winked, and Luke's fingers involuntarily tightened on the cup. "Travis already has a girlfriend."

What was he saying? Girlfriend or no girlfriend, Delaney was way too old to be potential sweetheart material for his son. Just as she was way too young for him.

"Maybe so. But boys will be boys and that little lady is a sure-enough eye catcher." Packy chuckled again, handed him his bill, and moved on to the next table.

Thanks a lot, buddy, for giving me another thing to worry about. He and Travis had talked before he'd left for school and it was mutually agreed that he owed Delaney an apology. He was proud of that boy—most of the time. Had he given his own dad so much grief as a teen?

Probably, if their current relationship was any indication. *Please, Lord, don't let me and Travis end up in the same place as I am with Dad.*

He glanced at the slip of paper Packy had given him, pulled cash from his wallet, then tucked the bills under his coffee cup. He needed to get going. He had more important things to do today than gawk at Delaney Marks. At any woman for that matter. But when he stepped outside, he couldn't help but scan the street for some sign of her.

She'd already disappeared.

He called to Rags, who'd been basking in the sun outside the café, then held open the door to his Chevy crew cab for the pup to make a running leap inside. While they kept office space here in town for the sake of convenience, Hunter's Hideaway was the heart and soul of Hunter Enterprises and he needed to get on back to home base.

The Hideaway, as most called the extensive, wooded property, had been in the family for six generations. In fact, it was the first business on the ridge, one started by his great-great-grandparents to accommodate the needs of hunters and back-country explorers in the early 1900's. Originally only a handful of cabins and a corral, it set the tone for a town that would soon follow. What would his ancestors think of it now? Boasting dozens of cabins, an inn with dining facilities, a general store, horse boarding, trail rides and more, it kept Luke's extended family busy around the clock.

He had a lot to get done today, but business with a potential hay supplier had required a breakfast meeting in town. It was already past nine now and he had more than enough to do to fill the coming hours.

"The day's getting away from us, Rags."

The dog sitting on the seat next to him perked his ears, tail wagging, and Luke gave him a hearty pat just as his cell phone rang.

"How goes it, Luke?" The voice of his old army comrade, Josh, echoed warmly across the miles.

About eight hundred miles, to be exact. If all went as hoped, he'd be able to drive the kids from Kansas back to Hunter Ridge for most major holidays and a few weeks each summer. But he wasn't ready to break that news to them just yet.

He inserted the key in the ignition and rolled down the window on the driver's side. "I guess congratulations are in order for that diploma a few weeks ago. Assuming you didn't get kicked out the door before graduation day, that is."

"Yeah, I finally got that university sheepskin. Feels good."

Both of his Kansas friends, a handful of years younger than Luke, had taken advantage of the GI Bill to further their education. That's something he'd intended to do. Where had time gotten to? But that lack of a degree was something he could remedy once he relocated to the Sunflower State.

"So what's up?" Luke's gaze roamed the street. Then, disgusted to realize he was looking for Delaney again, he turned away from the window.

"Vinnie thought we should touch base since we haven't talked in a while. See if you're on board to join up when that loan comes through."

"I am." Vinnie and Josh had a solid business plan—thanks to help from him—as well as a need for someone computer and numbers savvy to oversee the accounting of their growing enterprise. Several banks had turned them down on the expansion loan, but they had high hopes for this latest application. "Say the word."

"That's what we wanted to hear. I'll relay this to Vinnie, so have a good rest of your day, buddy."

"That's it?" He'd always teased Josh for his reticence, so unlike Vinnie, who'd talk your ear off. "You don't want to know what the weather is like here today or how my kids are doing?"

Josh laughed. "Report that in an email, okay? A short one."

Still smiling, Luke shut off the phone and

started up the truck. Those guys were top-notch. Definitely men he'd wanted watching his back in a combat zone. It would be great working with them again. Before school started, if all went well.

Not too far down the street he slowed to take the first of several curves snaking up the ridge through town and glanced toward the Artists' Co-op gallery. A natural stone building, it bumped up against a quilt shop on one side and an empty Hunter-owned storefront on the other.

No sign of Delaney.

He pressed his foot to the gas pedal and continued on, noting again how art-related studios and shops were filling in the empty properties more and more. He shook his head.

Luke rolled down the window on the passenger side, letting the cool air swirl in to hit him full in the face. Yeah, Uncle Doug's ex-wife, Charlotte, had started it all. That divorce had caused his uncle—the whole family—a heap of trouble.

"And you know what, buddy?" He glanced at Rags. "She not only had the gall to sell and lease to outsiders the properties her lawyers wrested away from Uncle Doug, she made sure she got them into the hands of those she knew would most stick in the craw of the community."

His grip tightened on the wheel. One artist soon became two. Then three. And four… What if by a freak turn of events Sunshine Carston beat his mother during the town council elections? While the council had cautiously addressed the demands of that growing community, they'd never before had one of them in their midst.

What if Delaney Marks got involved in the campaign? He'd tried to warn her off that first day when he'd caught a glimpse of Sunshine's flier in her possession. But with her committing the kids to that Mason house deal, he didn't put a whole lot of confidence in her personal judgment.

"Don't borrow trouble," he said aloud, slowing to drive down a graveled, tree-lined stretch of road that led to home. Sun dappled through the needled branches of the towering pines, a jay called out, and the familiar scent of the forest wafted through the open windows. He relaxed his hands on the steering wheel, determined not to dwell on the consequences of Aunt Char's vindictive betrayal of the family she'd married into. There was nothing he could do about that. Water under the bridge.

But he might yet be able to steer Ms. Marks away from local politics. And possibly even get her to recognize that another project would be more suitable than bending over backward to assist the Masons.

"Your workmanship shows much promise. But it's not quite there yet."

A wave of icy cold washed through Delaney as she stared into the keen black-brown eyes of

Sunshine Carston, manager of the Hunter Ridge Artists' Cooperative.

They were seated across from each other at a small oak table, the wood-trimmed display cases around them glinting invitingly in the soft light. Oil, acrylic, pastels and watercolor paintings, as well as wood and hammered copper designs, adorned walls or free-standing easels. Pottery and sculpted pieces joined a wide array of ceramic tiles, blown glass, and handmade leather handbags and belts. But, as always, it had been the jewelry in the glass cases that drew her the moment she'd stepped through the gallery's doors.

Swallowing back the lump forming in her throat, she prayed Ms. Carston—Sunshine, she'd told Delaney to call her—wouldn't perceive the wrenching impact of her point-blank pronouncement.

"I... I understand."

But she didn't. Her friends loved her rings and bracelets. Earrings. Charms. They said she should try to sell them, that maybe she could eventually earn a living doing what she loved most. Hadn't Luke Hunter, a total stranger, even said her work was nice? No, not merely nice. Very nice.

Luke. A knot twisted in her stomach at the thought of the handsome widower. While an unexpected negative response to her artistic efforts was a kick in the gut, this wasn't a tragedy like he and his children had suffered. Still suffered, for how could you ever recover from such a blow? With considerable effort, she refocused her thoughts on Sunshine, attempting to keep things in perspective.

But, to her shame, she failed miserably. How sure she'd been that her efforts would be welcomed, that she'd soon have a foot in the door to a future she could get excited about.

Studying Delaney's sampling of jewelry displayed against a sweep of dark velvet fabric, Sunshine brushed back her raven-black hair. Cut at an angle, shoulder-length in front and slightly shorter in back, it emphasized her high cheekbones, straight nose and a smooth, warm-toned complexion. Native American ancestry? She didn't look much older than Delaney, but there was something about the self-assured way she carried herself and looked at you, as if she could see right into your soul, that made Delaney feel about ten years old.

"How long did you say you've been working with silver? Since high school?" Obviously Sunshine doubted that anyone could have been making jewelry since a teen and have their work riddled with the flaws her experienced eyes must see.

Delaney clasped her hands tightly in her lap. "We made silver rings in high school art class. I loved it and have been making silver, beaded, and other kinds of jewelry ever since."

A kitchen table hobbyist. That's what Dwayne had dismissively called her.

A slight crease formed between Sunshine's brows as she again picked up one of the rings and tilted it in the lamplight. She tapped a blunt, unpolished fingernail on the inside of the ring. "See this seam? The bump?"

Delaney nodded. She'd worked hard on that one, trying to smooth out the solder without weakening the joint. Only an expert eye would have seen it as a flaw.

"And this?" Sunshine pointed to the setting. "This is too prominent, too fragile. Not organically incorporated into the design. It could easily catch on something, break off and the wearer would lose the stone."

Numb, Delaney nodded.

"Which is another thing..." Sunshine set the ring back on the velvet. "You need to upgrade the quality of your gemstones. I would also suggest something other than the turquoise you've used here if you want to stand out from the Native American artists."

Delaney was familiar with the work of those appearing in Arizona park and roadside stands, in shops and in exclusive galleries throughout the Southwest. The latter were award-winning, highly collectible artists. While awed by their talent, she'd never considered herself to be a competitor and had deliberately not imitated traditional native designs.

"I don't make jewelry full-time, of course." How pathetic her pieces now looked lying there under the illuminating brilliance of a gooseneck lamp. "I work it in around my job when I can."

Shut up, Delaney. Stop sounding as though you're making excuses for inferior work. Why hadn't she listened to Aunt Jen and Dwayne and not put herself through this embarrassment? But oh, no, she'd been certain they were wrong.

After what seemed an excruciatingly long moment, Sunshine again looked up from where she'd continued to study the jewelry. "What do you do for a living?"

Delaney lifted her chin slightly. "Computer programming."

The corners of Sunshine's lips lifted, her eyes warming. "No wonder you need a creative outlet."

"I enjoy the challenge." And she did. Most of the time. Not like Dwayne did, though, who lived and breathed programming and couldn't understand her need for anything else. But Aunt Jen had urged her on her career path, and since her aunt had been the one paying the bills… "But my heart has always been with the fine arts."

The other woman met her gaze in sympathy. "Which can be a rocky road if you hope to support yourself at it."

"No immediate plans to." Delaney forced a

laugh, as if to prove to Sunshine that she hadn't expected anything like that. But she had. Drawing comfort from the faint scent of oil paints and leather, she reluctantly glanced toward the glass cases where two women were excitedly examining the jewelry. Nothing of her own would be joining those beautifully arranged displays this summer.

"I don't want to take up any more of your time. You have customers." With a quick, apologetic smile, she rose to her feet. "Thank you for meeting with me."

Surprise lit Sunshine's eyes. Did people who were turned down for the co-op argue with her? Plead their case? But too clearly there was jewelry like she was making…and then there was *fine* jewelry that this gallery featured.

Sunshine stood as well, watching as Delaney carefully returned her silver pieces to a velvet-lined box which she then slipped into her portfolio.

"Please don't leave here feeling as if your work holds no value. Even at your present skill level, you could make reasonable sales." Sunshine folded her arms, her sharp black-brown eyes assessing. "Your designs have a light, feminine touch that many beginning to work with silver are incapable of producing. Often newbie pieces have a clunky, even masculine feel to them even though they're meant for women."

"Thank you." But the approving words did little to appease the sick feeling in Delaney's stomach. "I'd hoped to test the waters this summer, to see if my work might be saleable at the co-op on consignment, but I realize now that my coming here was premature."

Much too premature.

Sunshine walked her to the door. "Have you given any thought to working with a mentor? Another silversmith? It's something you might want to consider. If you decide that's a path you'd like to pursue, come see me again. I may be able to help you work something out with a local artist."

"Unfortunately, I'm only here for the summer to work with a church youth group."

Together Delaney and Sunshine stepped outside under the gallery's striped awning.

"Thanks again and…" Delaney nodded to a flyer taped to the front door of the gallery. "I hope all goes well for the town council run."

Sunshine laughed. "It's a long shot. The oldtimers are entrenched here. But the growing number of artists making this a home need a voice in local government. We need support to grow our businesses and carve out a comfortable niche in a town dominated by hunters, horsemen and hikers who tend to eye us with suspicion."

"Why suspicion?"

Sunshine's smile faltered. "We're called 'outsiders' by many and 'aliens' by some, as if oil paint, pottery kilns and other artistic tools might pollute the macho, outdoorsy atmosphere. It's been an uphill battle all the way."

"If you don't mind me asking, why did you settle in Hunter Ridge? Why not someplace more welcoming?"

Something Delaney couldn't read flickered through the other woman's eyes, then quickly shuttered. Sunshine motioned to the shady street before them. "Cool summers are inviting to shoppers from the Phoenix area. That can be a big business draw if we had the opportunity to develop it more. The town's floundered for quite a few years. Its focus on one aspect for their economy—outdoorsmen—has left it vulnerable."

"There's the overall economic hit this country has taken, too," Delaney added. Canyon Springs had been impacted as well.

"Right. Over time the population here has dropped to under two thousand. Businesses have closed." Sunshine surveyed the buildings along the street. "The plus side is there's now more commercial space available. But even with prices jacked up—to keep us out, I suspect—property is less expensive than in more flourishing towns like Sedona or even Canyon Springs."

"It sounds as if Hunter Ridge is the perfect spot for potential artistic projects."

"It is. If you're interested in learning more, come by tonight for our first town council campaign meeting. Seven o'clock. Here."

"Thanks." It sounded like a worthwhile cause. But Delaney wasn't making any commitments. Not only had Luke Hunter warned her about getting involved in local politics but, with her artistic self-confidence shot to smithereens, she wasn't up to hobnobbing with the established artisans of Hunter Ridge.

No, tonight would find her packing up her silversmithing supplies and stuffing them in a dark corner of the closet—and trying to come up with a way to convince Luke Hunter that the project she'd selected was the best choice for the youth group.

Chapter Five

"So this is it?"

Delaney cringed inwardly as Luke, hands placed on his slim, jeans-clad hips, raised a questioning brow at the matted layers of pine needles and pinecones littering the front yard of the house that was to be the youth group's summer project. His skeptical eyes took in the broken-down fence and crumbling concrete walkway. A cracked window.

If only she'd had the opportunity to see the place the first time by herself, not under the scrutiny of an already dubious parent, albeit a handsome one. Just before noon that Tuesday morning, following a trip to see Aunt Jen, she'd picked up the keys from High Country Hope Ministries, only to be intercepted by Luke who'd invited himself along for a preview of the place.

No, the two-story house wasn't exactly a mansion, but at least from the outside it appeared to have good bones. Once cleaned up, it would make a cozy dwelling for family members who had been separated for much too long.

A happy home for twelve-year-old Samantha Mason.

She looked Luke in the eye, determined not to let him discourage her. She'd grown up in a series of houses not much better cared for than this one, so she knew how others would negatively judge it.

"The youth group won't be painting the outside, will they?" He frowned at the peeling paint high up on the exterior, obviously picturing rickety ladders and a 911 call.

"No. Hope Ministries contracted with a licensed roofer and painter who have the scaffolding and ladders for that. Electrical and plumbing have been checked out. This isn't a remodel, the kids will only clean up and paint the inside." Would that satisfy him? She motioned around the spacious treed lot. "They'll be in charge of the yard work, too, of course. Sprucing things up, planting flowers."

Luke reached down to pat Rags, who'd stuck like glue to his master's side, then straightened. "Looks as if it's going to take more than a pot of flowers to get this yard in shape. From the depth of those pine needles, I'm guessing nobody's raked in years. That's a fire hazard in these parts."

He wasn't telling her anything she didn't already know.

Luke motioned toward the side of the house

and together, along with Rags, they walked the perimeter of the structure, taking in the chipped paint, a warped window frame, a detached garage. She couldn't help but sneak an occasional peek at him, but his expression was unreadable, almost as if he knew she hoped he'd give the project the go-ahead and intended to make her wait for his final verdict.

"Pretty badly neglected," he said at last, but she didn't allow her shoulders to slump at his statement. "I remember the guy who lived here when I was a kid. I used to feed his cat and water his plants when he was out of town."

"You did?" As she'd assumed, Luke was a hometown boy. His wife had probably been his high school sweetheart, too. But were his memories of the house and its previous owner good ones that might sway his decision? "Min Chambers, the head of Hope Ministries, said it belonged to an elderly gentleman."

"Bachelor Bob, we called him."

"Min said when he died, the place got tangled up in a feud between his out-of-town nieces and nephews. Until the legalities were straightened out, the house sat vacant before it was put on the market. That's been three or four years, but obviously it wasn't well cared for even before that."

"Let's take a look inside."

Before she could launch into a list of reasons not to, a car pulled up in front of the house and five of the youth group teens, including Travis and his girlfriend, hopped out and joined them.

"We saw your truck, Dad." Luke's son put his hands on his hips much in the same manner as his father as he scanned the house. "Kind of run-down, isn't it?"

Pushing aside her own misgivings, Delaney offered an optimistic smile. Even on an always-tight budget, her folks had turned neglected houses similar to this one into homes, and she knew they could, too. "What it lacks right now is tender loving care."

Travis snorted. "TLC? Are you kidding? I sure hope the inside is better than the outside."

Luke cast her a look that said he agreed with his son's candid evaluation. "We were preparing to check it out, Trav. Care to join us?"

This was *not* how an introduction to the house was to have taken place. She'd wanted to get a feel for the work to be done, then present a plan to the kids and parents along with a guided tour. She'd certainly have done advance cleanup on her own.

Nevertheless, with Luke and the five teens right behind her, she stepped up on the covered porch, opened the screen door and inserted a key in the dead bolt. Taking a steadying breath, she pushed open the door. *Please, Lord, let the inside be better than the outside.*

It wasn't.

"Ugh." Travis slipped past her, hand in hand

with Scottie, whose nose was crinkled in disgust as they stepped into the shadowed entryway, the long-shut-up space somehow still smelling faintly of stale cigarette.

Luke gave a low whistle as they moved into the adjoining living room, an open spindled staircase overlooking the space. "This used to be a nice place. Not fancy, but I had no idea Bachelor Bob lived like this in his later years."

Delaney reached for the wall switch, illuminating the room and her heart plummeted even further. In all honesty, the house had the appearance of a secondhand shop that had been hit by a tornado. Furniture was arranged haphazardly. Newspapers and magazines were piled up on a sagging sofa and empty soda cans littered the floor. Ashtrays overflowed. Dog or cat hair clung to the blades of the overhead fan, and light filtering through the heavy, ratty-looking drapes revealed peeling wallpaper and a stained carpet that had seen better days.

"Yuck." Red-haired Nelson eyed the room with revulsion.

Cautiously picking a path through the debris, they ventured to another room, its built-in corner cabinetry suggesting it had served as a dining room even though no table or chairs filled the space, and then peered into the dimly lit kitchen.

"They want this place livable by August?" Kendrick gazed doubtfully around the room. Linoleum buckled, the cabinets needed fresh paint and scarred countertops begged to be replaced. Food-encrusted dishes were stacked in the sink, likely from when Bachelor Bob left them there. "Try August a decade from now."

Under Luke's disapproving gaze, Delaney turned to the dining room window to push aside the drapes. With a gasp she leaped back as the curtain rod pulled loose from the wall, the weight of the heavy lined fabric sending her stumbling into Luke's sturdy frame. How embarrassing. But she nevertheless managed to smile up at him as his strong hands set her upright for the second time in a week. "See what a bit of sunshine can do?"

Travis shook his head. "Yeah, now you can see the spiderwebs and the gunk on the floor."

"Don't look in the half bath back there, either," warned Nelson's twin as he rejoined them. "I checked it out. Talk about gross."

A corner of Travis's lip curled. "Not even the Masons will want to move in here."

"They will when we're done with it." Delaney determinedly motioned toward the kitchen. "Imagine what it will look like with new flooring, painted cabinets, and the walls a creamy yellow. Cheerful curtains will go above the sink and a cute oak table will fit in over there."

Kendrick grimaced. "Imagination is about as good as it's going to get."

"I like it." Everyone turned to the curly-haired Sybil who up until now had trailed behind the others, remaining silent, her arms wrapped tightly around herself as if unwilling to touch anything. "It's kind of like Charlie Brown's Christmas tree, don't you think? All it needs is love."

"Love it all you want, Syb." Travis gave her a mocking smile. "You'll have to love it enough for the rest of us, because we're not cleaning anybody's disgusting house."

"I like it, too, now that I'm getting used to it." Scottie shot her boyfriend a challenging look. "It's like one of those places they fix up on TV. You know, the before and after shows."

"It is, isn't it?" Nelson looked around the room with renewed interest.

Delaney's spirits lifted. "It is."

Travis punched his father lightly in the shoulder. "What do *you* think, Dad?"

Luke gazed around the room, taking in the details. Had he noticed the quality woodwork around the windows and doors? The home's potential? She waited with bated breath.

"Well…" he said at long last. "It has character."

Travis grinned at his friends, confident his father was about to put the kibosh on the project.

Luke turned to Delaney. "This place has been closed up for quite a few years. If rodents are lurking about, there could be a risk no parent would be willing to take."

"They've had it checked out. Clean bill of health." Thank goodness Hope Ministries had seen to that already.

"There's a lot of work to be done here in a limited amount of time." Luke again assessed the space. "But the interior appears to be doable. Good old-fashioned manual labor."

Hope sparking, Delaney watched him intently. The kids seemed divided. Luke's opinion could sway the final decision either way.

A clearly dismayed Travis stared at his dad. "You're saying we have to take this on?"

"I'll leave that decision up to the youth group." Luke cast a questioning look at the teens even though Sunday night he hadn't hesitated to communicate that he thought her idea was a bad one. Was he so confident that they'd nix the project that he could leave the kids to make their own decision?

Travis triumphantly shot his hand high above his head. "All in favor of ditching this place raise your hand."

Without hesitation, Kendrick seconded the motion with a wave of his upstretched arm. But Sybil crossed her arms and Scottie pointedly slipped her hands behind her back. Nelson, avoiding Travis's glare, stared at the floor.

"Come on, dude." Travis's tone was that of someone used to giving orders and having them followed. "Don't tell me you can hardly wait to scrub bathrooms for the Masons."

Delaney held her breath.

"Of course not, but…" Nelson met his friend's gaze. "But what if that's exactly what God wants me to do?"

"Come on, you're letting the girls sway you."

"No, I'm not. I'm thinking about something Jesus said. You know, about how if we help someone in need, it's as though we were doing it for Him." He turned to his twin. "If Jesus was the one moving in here, would *you* clean it up for Him?"

Sensing the direction this might be headed, Travis firmly grasped Kendrick's still-upraised arm to hold it steady. But the redheaded boy tugged away and slowly lowered his hand.

"Yeah, I guess I would."

The girls clapped, ignoring a scowling Travis as their bright eyes met Delaney's. She glanced toward Luke. So that was it? He wasn't going to try to talk them out of it? Insist that other parents weigh in or that the rest of the youth group vote?

Nelson glanced at his watch. "Hey, we'd better get moving. Lunch break's almost over. We don't want detentions this close to the end of the year."

Tomorrow was the last day of school and next weekend they could get the youth project started.

Nelson's announcement was enough to get the kids out the door and, when they'd departed, Delaney turned cautiously to Luke.

* * *

"So you're good with this?" Delaney looked up at him with hopeful eyes. Pretty, appealing eyes.

Did it much matter what he thought? With Lois and Garrett from the church on board, would she defer to his opinion? Not likely. But it wasn't so much about the effort it would take. Manual labor wouldn't hurt any of the kids. It was about the Masons.

"There's a lot more work to be done here than I think you realize."

"It's doable. You said so yourself."

"Given all hands on deck day in and day out, sure. But you could be biting off more than you can chew."

Her chin lifted. "Garrett thinks that with the kids pitching in most Saturdays and a few other days here and there, we can do it with room to spare."

Since when had the preacher acquired project management savvy?

"That's just it. I'm not going to order Travis or Anna to take part if they don't want to. I doubt many parents will either once they learn that this place is for Benton and Lizzie Mason."

Moving to stand inside the foyer, he glanced up the wooden staircase to the second floor. He should probably check that out, too, but didn't imagine it was in much better condition than the main floor. Structurally, though, the house seemed to be sound. The project would mainly be de-junking and deep cleaning. Repair and cosmetic work.

Who'd have thought old Bachelor Bob, always shaved and spotlessly dressed, lived in such squalor? Had no one made sure he was doing okay? Or, more likely, had the sometimes stubborn old guy refused assistance?

Joining him in the foyer, Delaney stepped close with an attention-getting poke in the arm, her eyes troubled. "Do people hate the Masons that much? So much that they don't want them to have decent living conditions? To be together as a family?"

"Nobody hates anybody." Where'd she get that idea? "But this is a town where most people take pride in doing whatever needs to be done to provide for their families. We choose to hold up our head. And if we can't make a go of it here, we move on, not expecting handouts from others who sacrificed to get whatever they've managed to attain."

Which was exactly why, if it worked out, he and his children would be heading to Kansas soon. He couldn't tolerate being dependent on his folks for much longer. A man had his pride.

"The Masons have had some setbacks. They need help getting back on their feet."

He gave her a level look, trying not to notice how her hair glimmered in the dim light, framing the soft oval of her face. "I doubt they've ever stood on their own two feet. From what I've seen, few in the fine arts around here are able to support themselves with their art. Most have to supplement with other means of income."

"But—"

"The Masons think they live in an age where a wealthy patron—or the hardworking citizens around them—should put a roof over their head and feed their five kids while they dabble in their art. I'm not convinced you can help people who make no effort to help themselves."

Sadness touched her features. "Kids shouldn't be punished because of their parents."

"Nobody's punishing anyone."

She tilted her head thoughtfully, a curious light now filling her eyes. "What do *you* do for a living, Luke?"

He shifted, uncomfortable with the abrupt change in topic. Where was she going with this? "I do bookkeeping for Hunter Enterprises."

"Have you always done that?"

"No. And no, it's not my dream job. But I do it because it needs to be done and it provides for my family." And he'd already decided that it wasn't enough, that changes needed to be made.

"What *is* your dream job?" She gave him a pointed look.

"I—" Did he even have one anymore? He'd been in the army quite a few years, targeting what he thought would be a lifetime career. But when Marsha's mental health became an issue, his focus wavered. And after…after she'd chosen to leave him, he'd switched gears to be there for his kids. No, it hadn't been an easy decision to leave the army. Nor was choosing now to leave Hunter Ridge. "This isn't about me, Delaney."

She continued to study him. "But you won't try to stop the youth group from working on the project, will you?"

He stepped back, away from the faint sweet scent of her.

"Like I said, I'll let my kids decide for themselves." It would be a no-go for Travis. But he didn't want peer pressure from Sybil and Scottie to push Anna into something she didn't want to do. That oldest Mason boy had picked on her at times. "I can't speak for the parents of the other members of the youth group."

Delaney's narrowed eyes implied he could influence them if he chose to. As a matter of fact, he could—and would—had the Masons not been the intended recipients of the group's hard work.

"I guess we wait and see, then," she concluded. "But we need to get started by Saturday. I'll contact the other parents and invite them to see the place Friday evening."

Not until Friday? Was that so she could clean up the property herself in hopes of swaying opinion? Inwardly he groaned. Should he offer to help get the beyond-repair furniture and junk moved out?

She sure couldn't haul it away on that bicycle of hers that she'd been tooling around town on the past few days.

Then again, Garrett had probably offered his assistance. From the impression he got when Delaney first arrived, Garrett likely had designs on her. Couldn't blame him. She'd make a better pastor's wife than a gal who Luke suspected he'd not quite gotten over.

With a wistful look, Delaney made a sweeping motion toward the living room. "Hopefully we can—"

That's when he noticed.

"Hey, what happened to the rings?"

She glanced self-consciously at her hands, then tucked them behind her, avoiding his gaze.

"Did you get them placed at the Artists' Co-op?"

She shook her head. "It didn't work out."

"It wasn't worth your time?"

"It wasn't worth the Co-op's time." Her cheeks dimpled as if somehow finding humor in that. "I didn't meet their standards."

He'd heard similar self-critical assumptions too many times from Anna when things didn't go as she'd hoped. "Maybe your jewelry didn't meet their standards, but don't say *you* didn't."

Startled eyes looked up at his firm reprimand. "Okay, my jewelry didn't meet their standards. It didn't even make it to the jury phase. In fact, Sunshine Carston wouldn't accept my application fee and paperwork for membership, so at least I didn't suffer the humiliation of an official rejection by all the members of the Co-op."

Leave it to Sunshine to trample somebody's dreams.

"It's my experience that Ms. Carston is an opinionated young woman. She's not always right even though she thinks she is. I thought your rings were real nice."

"Thanks, but I'll survive. It was a whim anyway."

Again avoiding his probing gaze, she slipped past him, out the door and on to the porch where Rags awaited. Luke followed, pulling the door closed behind him.

"You were excited about it last week. I say if your work didn't make the cut, step up and make it happen."

"What do you mean?"

"Put more effort into it. You know, practice makes perfect."

Irritation flashed in her eyes, but when she turned away to insert the key in the dead-bolt lock, her words came lightly. "Like I said. No biggie. There won't be time for that nonsense with the youth project filling my time anyway."

She might sound indifferent, but he didn't miss that the deliberately nonchalant tone masked deep disappointment, not only annoyance with him. He could tell by the set of her jaw, as well, that the subject was closed and further discussion unwelcome.

She stepped off the porch, Rags close at her heels, then knelt down to hold the dog's furry face between her hands. Roughing up his fur, she dodged his tongue with a laugh, as if without a care in the world. As though her artistic ambitions didn't matter. Had never mattered.

Never one to be praised for his perceptiveness and sensitivity, Luke nevertheless knew better. But why did he hate it so much that Sunshine had squelched Delaney's dream? And why was a plan already formulating in his head?

Chapter Six

"Isn't this adorable?" Delaney's longtime friend, Paris Perslow, soon to be Paris Hawk, lifted down an oversize, stuffed bear from a Timbertop Gift Shop shelf. "Do you think Deron is too old for it?"

Deron was the six-year-old nephew of Paris's fiancé and, if all continued as planned, he'd be their adopted son in the not-too-distant future. From the way her gray eyes lit up, Paris had obviously already fallen in love with the furry critter. Just as she had with Deron.

"Every kid needs a stuffed bear at some time in their life. From what you've told me about his background, I doubt he's ever had one."

"Then I'll get it." With a satisfied smile, Paris held the bear out at arms' length. "This little guy can keep Deron company while Cody and I are away on our honeymoon."

Periodically pausing to peruse the tiny shop's mountain-themed wares, together they made their way to the checkout counter where an auburn-haired young woman rang up the sale. She glanced at Delaney almost shyly.

"You're working with the Christ's Church youth group this summer, aren't you?"

"I am. I'm Delaney Marks. This is my friend Paris. And you are…"

"Lacy Cox. I was at church when they introduced you." She slipped the bear into a large, decorative shopping bag, his face peeking over the top, and handed it to Paris. "Welcome to Hunter Ridge."

"Thank you. I've been here such a short time, but already love the town and the kids in the youth group."

Delaney turned to scan the store, then turned back to Lacy. "You wouldn't happen to know if there's anywhere in town that carries quality men's leather wallets, would you? Paris is trying to find a gift for her fiancé's best man."

Lacy smiled at Paris. "You're getting married soon?"

"A few weeks."

"Congratulations." Then her dark eyes narrowed in thought. "We lost our men's clothing store a few years ago. But try the Echo Ridge Outpost. It's just down the road, past Cousin Cathy's Closet. They specialize in outdoor gear, but have a bunch of other stuff, too, like leather goods."

Delaney exchanged a look with Paris and her friend nodded.

"We'll check it out. Thanks, Lacy. It's been good meeting you."

On the street, the two friends paused to get their bearings, and Delaney pointed toward where she thought the recommended store would be. "It's getting close to lunchtime, but should we first go see if that store carries wallets?"

Paris didn't respond and Delaney caught her staring down the street in the opposite direction.

"Paris? Should we—"

"Who is *that*?"

Delaney tracked her line of vision. Then her heart gave a jerk of recognition. Luke. Sleeves rolled up to display impressive biceps, he was unloading boxes from the back of his pickup outside the Hunter Enterprises office.

"That's Luke Hunter."

Paris turned to her, openmouthed. "You haven't even been here a full week and you actually know that guy? And you didn't think it important enough to tell me about him?"

Warmth permeated Delaney's cheeks and she prayed it wasn't translating into a telltale blush. "He has teenagers in the youth group."

The light in Paris's eyes dimmed and her mouth took a downturn. "Okay. I get it. Married. Bummer."

"Actually…he's not. He's a widower."

Her friend again cast an interested look in Luke's direction. "Not for long, I imagine."

"Six years, I've been told."

"You're kidding. A gorgeous guy like that has been running loose for six years?"

"Stop staring at him." Delaney uttered the terse words under her breath. "He might see you."

Too late.

Luke spotted them, recognized Delaney and lifted a hand in greeting. No smile. Heart hammering, Delaney waved back, then he returned to his work.

"I want to meet him." Paris took a determined step forward, but Delaney gripped her arm.

"No, not now."

"Why not?"

"Mr. Hunter and I..." What could she say that wouldn't encourage her friend to interrogate her further?

Paris arched a brow, sensing Delaney's reluctance to be drawn into discussion. "Mr. Hunter and you...what?"

Delaney tugged on her arm, forcing her friend in the direction of the Echo Ridge Outpost. "We're not exactly seeing eye to eye on the youth group project right now. In fact, he's dead set against it and being rather uncooperative."

"What's his problem with it?"

"He thinks the family we're fixing up the house for is undeserving. He—and apparently many people in town—bear an animosity toward the growing community of artists, which both the mother and father of this family are a part of."

"And you."

"Me?"

"You're an artist, too, remember."

"I haven't been invited into the inner circle, remember?" She'd already explained, in excruciating detail, that humiliating meeting with the manager of the Artists' Co-op.

"You should go to one of the campaign meetings you were telling me about. Maybe you can earn brownie points."

Delaney shook her head. If her craftsmanship hadn't won Sunshine over, she certainly wouldn't try to finagle her way in through the back door.

They paused outside Echo Ridge Outpost where Delaney looked doubtfully at the display window filled with hunting and camping gear. "I'm not sure this place will have what you're looking for, but I guess it's worth a try."

They'd barely stepped inside when a friendly male voice called out. "How can I help you ladies?"

Delaney's eyes widened as a thirtyish-looking man with collar-length blond hair and piercing blue eyes approached. Jeans, work boots and a slate-blue river driver's shirt painted the picture of a man at home in the outdoors. That image was completed by a shotgun held casually in one hand, its barrel pointed, thankfully, at the floor.

"We're looking for men's wallets. For a gift."

"Right this way, then." He led them to a display

case near the cash register where he gently placed the gun atop it.

"Not loaded," he assured with a smile that could send the North Pole into meltdown. Then he slipped behind the case and pulled out a tray of leather billfolds and silver money clips.

Paris set the bear bag on the floor by her feet, then examined the display. "These are beautiful."

"Locally made and one of a kind," the clerk assured.

"What do you think?" Paris picked up one and ran her finger across the skillful tooling. "Do any of these strike you in particular, Delaney?"

"Delaney?" Curiosity lit the clerk's eyes. "Delaney Marks?"

"Yes." Should she know him?

"That's not a first name you hear too often." He thrust out his hand. "Sawyer Banks, owner of this establishment. Good to meet you."

She shook his hand and introduced Paris. "How do you know my name?"

"I heard you're working for Christ's Church this summer and that you're a jewelry maker as well."

Small towns. Everyone probably knew her shoe size and what brand of toothpaste she used, too. "I dabble in silverwork and also beaded jewelry."

He motioned around the store. "As you can see, I could use something more feminine in here to cater to discriminating ladies. Do you ever sell on consignment? Fifty-fifty?"

Fifty-fifty? Was that the going rate for consignment sales at most places? She had no idea. But with her jewelry priced as that of a novice, it probably wouldn't cover the cost of her supplies, let alone her time.

"Thanks, but I'm still a beginner. Not quite there yet." As tempting as his offer was, after what Sunshine had said about her jewelry, wouldn't that almost be like trying to dupe customers into accepting inferior work?

Paris nudged her. "You should do it, Delaney."

"I don't—"

"You have to begin somewhere, don't you? Few writers start out on the *New York Times* bestsellers list."

"Well, no, but…"

"Bring your stuff by," Sawyer urged. "Let me take a look at it and pick out a few pieces. We'll write up a contract and get you started right here at the Outpost."

An outdoor gear shop? Wedged in among backpacks and shotguns? That wasn't exactly how she'd envisioned her professional debut.

"Come on, do it." Paris's eyes danced with excitement.

Butterflies bumping the walls of Delaney's stomach, she glanced up at Sawyer who nodded encouragingly.

"I… Okay, I guess."

Paris slipped her arm around her for a sideways hug. "This will be fun, Delaney."

Would it?

What if Sunshine heard she was doing this? In a town this small, she was certain to. Would she think that her advice to acquire a mentor and improve her skills had been kicked to the gutter by artistic arrogance? Then again, hadn't she said that even at this stage of her experience, Delaney could expect to make reasonable sales? Sunshine wouldn't have mentioned it had she not meant it, would she?

As if in a fog, her mind racing as she mentally inventoried the jewelry pieces she'd stuffed in a box only a few days ago, she observed as Paris selected a wallet for her fiancé's friend. Sale finalized, Sawyer sent them off with a reminder that he expected to see her work soon.

Outside and a short distance down the street, Paris and Delaney exchanged a glance and drew to a halt, then broke into laughter.

"Did that just happen? My jewelry is going to be sold on consignment in an outdoor gear shop?"

"Right next to the canteens and shotgun shells."

"I can't believe I'm doing this." Delaney squeezed her friend's arm. "I must be insane."

"No, no. This is good. A great marketing ploy."

"It is?"

"Of course. You know how diverse the merchandise is at Dix's Woodland Warehouse in Canyon Springs and what a wide variety of shoppers cross its threshold. Dix's takes stuff on consignment all the time. People who might not set foot in a jewelry store or art gallery see those items there and whip out the old credit card."

That was true. Owner Sharon Dixon Diaz wouldn't do that if it wasn't mutually advantageous to both her and the craftsmen she dealt with. People like Paris's future mother-in-law, for instance, who designed Christmas wreaths and other holiday decorations for sale there.

Paris lowered her voice to a whisper. "And think of the bonus."

"Bonus?" Delaney also kept her voice low.

"You know, an excuse to periodically drop in on Sawyer."

Delaney laughed softly. "You thought he was cute, too?"

"Are you kidding me? Those blue eyes and the way his hair dips across his forehead? Oh, my goodness. You may have to take up trapshooting this summer."

With another laugh, Delaney's voice returned to its normal tone. "I could do that!"

"You could do what?" Someone else intruded into their conversation.

Both of them started at the sound of the low male voice and turned to see Luke Hunter as he stepped out of the store behind them.

Chapter Seven

Pretty as a picture, the both of them. But from the look they exchanged, he'd have been better off to have minded his own business.

"Girl talk, Luke." Eyes dancing, Delaney smiled up at him, not hiding her pleasure that he'd joined them. "We're making plans for our summer."

Her friend looked as if she wanted to laugh.

"Paris," Delaney said, motioning to him, "I'd like you to meet one of the youth group parents, Luke Hunter, who also happens to be my landlord. Luke, this is my best friend, Paris Perslow. From Canyon Springs."

"Good to meet you, Paris."

The brunette studied him with open interest. "Likewise."

"Paris is getting married soon, so we've been shopping for a gift for her fiancé's best man."

He nodded toward her friend's shopping bag. "Into wildlife, is he?"

Paris laughed at the furry face peeping over the top. "Actually, this cute guy is for my fiancé's nephew. We got his best man a wallet."

With a sense of satisfaction, Luke noted that the smaller bag she lifted from the larger one carried an Outpost logo. Had Sawyer come through for him? He didn't dare ask. "A wallet's a good choice. Hard to slip a teddy bear into a back pocket."

"It is."

He glanced at Delaney, who was still smiling at him, and his heart did a slow rollover. He cleared his throat. "Well, I don't want to hold you ladies up if you're on a shopping mission."

"I think we're finished." Delaney looked to Paris for confirmation. "We're heading to lunch now. I want Paris to see the Log Cabin Café."

Luke nodded. "That teddy bear will feel right at home."

Paris smiled. "You can join us, too."

He cut another glance at Delaney, catching the surprised look she shot her friend. "Thanks, but I don't want to intrude on your day in town."

"You wouldn't be." Paris adjusted her grip on the shopping bag. "I'm looking forward to getting to know Delaney's Hunter Ridge friends this summer."

Delaney again flashed the smile that always set off warning bells in his head. Surprisingly, their differences over the project house never seemed to dim the openly interested look in her eyes for long. But he wasn't free to follow through on any attraction and it wasn't right to give her the impression that he might.

"I'm afraid I—"

Someone roughly bumped him from behind and he saw Garrett standing there, rocking on his heels and innocently gazing up at the cloudless blue sky. Nevertheless, he rewarded his cousin with a grateful smile. Saved by the bell, so to speak.

Garrett nodded to the ladies. Did his gaze linger a tad longer on the smiling Delaney? "Good morning. That wedding day is fast approaching, isn't it, Paris?"

"Almost here."

He turned to Luke. "Paris works part-time at Canyon Springs Christian when she's not showing properties to potential buyers and renters."

Luke nodded, putting two and two together. She must be one of the Perslows of Perslow Real Estate and Property Management. A prominent area family. For whatever reason, he hadn't gotten the impression that Delaney ran in those circles, but maybe he was mistaken. She'd said Paris was her best friend.

"This is the last day of school, isn't it, Luke?" At Luke's nod, Garrett said to Delaney, "So you should soon have plenty of worker bees available for the project. Will there be a kickoff tomorrow?"

"Not until Saturday." Her gaze flicked briefly to Luke. "That is, if the youth group parents approve once they see the place on Friday night."

A crease formed between Garrett's brows. "What's that about? Of course they'll be on board.

The youth project is a big deal every summer. Even when I was in high school."

"It looks as if the house may be in worse shape than anticipated, so it was suggested that parents should have an opportunity to weigh in. And then…" She paused, but didn't look at Luke. "There are concerns that there might be parental pushback due to the intended occupants."

She exchanged a quick glance with Paris. So she'd clued her friend in on the issues he'd brought to her attention.

Garrett grimaced. "You're kidding. What grinch told you that?"

Luke cleared his throat. May as well fess up. "This one."

"Why am I not surprised?" Garrett shook his head. "Well, get over it, cuz. This project is no different than any other that's been done in the past. It's a good cause. And one the church has committed to."

Luke crossed his arms. "I think it would be a good idea to—"

"I agree." Delaney looked him in the eye, then back at Garrett. "I want parents to feel ownership in this project. To encourage their kids to be a part of it. So I've arranged with High Country Hope Ministries to have someone on staff be present Friday night at the project house to answer questions. Your presence would be much appreciated, too, Garrett."

"I'll check my calendar and if it's clear, I'll be there." He cut a disgruntled look at Luke. "But I'm not sure this meeting provides added value. It delays your start by several days."

"I believe the head of Hope Ministries said you've seen the place. So you know the condition it's in. I admit, I was taken aback when Luke and I saw it for the first time yesterday."

"It's definitely going to take a lot of sweat and elbow grease."

"So you can see," she continued in a reasonable tone of voice, not pointing an accusing finger at Luke, "why having a few days to make decisions on where the junk will be moved or disposed of may be a blessing in disguise."

Garrett raised his hands in surrender. "Whatever you say. I'm not going to argue with a determined woman."

And a pretty one. Even though Garrett hadn't said it aloud, no doubt he was thinking it. Did he notice how her hair shimmered in the light? Did his fingers itch to reach out and touch it?

"When Paris heads home after lunch," Delaney said, "I plan to go over there and get organized. Maybe start sorting things."

Garrett nodded. "I can stop by this afternoon, too."

Like that came as any surprise? This guy was so transparent it wasn't even funny.

Give your cousin a break, Hunter.

Luke's conscience nagged. Garrett might come across as happy-go-lucky most of the time, but life hadn't been all sunshine and roses for him, either. And being a pastor of a church without a helpmate at his side, well, that had to be rough. Lonely.

And Luke understood lonely.

Garrett looked at him expectantly. "Are you available this afternoon?"

"I'm afraid not. I have to get back to the Hideaway." There was no point in horning in on Garrett's time with Delaney. Although, knowing Garrett's standards for himself, he'd make sure he and Delaney weren't alone at the house, unchaperoned for long.

How *did* a single pastor manage to pull off a courtship and keep tongues from wagging? As God's representative, he had more pressure than most to protect his reputation. How did he make sure there were no false accusations of misconduct by women he encountered on a day-to-day basis?

But sympathetic to Garrett's plight or not, Luke wasn't volunteering for chaperone duty. And his reluctance had nothing to do with Delaney Marks, whose eyes met his with an unsettling shadow of disappointment.

"And this," Lizzie Mason said on Friday morning, proudly draping her arm around the preteen at her side, "is Samantha."

Stunned by the similarities to her younger

sister, Delaney shook the girl's hand as she took in the ponytail and slash of dark brows contrasting with the golden hair. Coltish long legs. A wide, shy smile.

Samantha would one day be a beauty, as no doubt Tiffany would have been. What would it be like to now have a grown-up sister to laugh with? And share secrets? Would she have married by now and made Delaney sister-in-law to some great guy? Maybe even an aunt?

"It's good to meet you, Samantha."

The girl met her gaze briefly, then thrust her hands into her back jeans pockets. Just like Tiff used to do.

Min Chambers, head of High Country Hope Ministries who had helped sort and box Bachelor Bob's remaining possessions the past day and a half, placed her hands on her ample hips, a warm, motherly woman who had a gift for making those around her feel comfortable. "I know it's hard to envision with these boxes stacked around, but what do you think of your new room, Sam?"

"I like it. Especially that window seat."

The bedroom was tiny, but featured windows on two sides of the knotty pine walls. As the only daughter in the Mason household, it was an ideal space for a tween's getaway.

"What's your favorite color, Samantha?" Like Tiffany, it had to be a shade of purple. That is, if she'd personally picked out the somewhat faded sweatshirt she was wearing. But it wouldn't hurt to have that confirmed before Delaney did a bit of shopping.

"Lavender and pink."

"Then we'll make sure your room features those colors." Lois at the church said the women's ministry would supply new bedding, but Delaney intended to include a few other matching items near and dear to a teenage girl's heart. Rugs. Lamps. Pillows. Posters.

Samantha's smile widened as she exchanged a look of excitement with her mother.

"Well, we need to be going." Lizzie moved toward the door, and Delaney was again struck by how much younger Benton Mason's wife was than what she'd imagined the mother of five to be.

Early thirties, with a generous smile and light brown, French-braided hair, the expression in her eyes nevertheless held a wariness that tugged at Delaney's heart. The look suggested Lizzie had reasons to not trust the world around her.

"Min wanted me to bring Samantha by to see the house," she continued. "And I wanted to thank all of you for what you're doing. I—" She stopped abruptly, as if momentarily overcome by emotion. "This means so much to me."

Delaney stepped forward to give her slim frame a hug. "We're happy to be able to help. I understand what it's like to be separated from those you love. I know how hard it is."

She didn't know what it was like to be separated from a husband or a child. But it couldn't be much easier than what she'd been through herself.

Still somewhat shaken by the similarities between the Mason girl and her little sister, Delaney saw Min and the Masons to the front door. Waving goodbye, she noticed a familiar pickup now parked on the street behind Garrett's SUV. Luke was here?

Her heart doing an unexpected pirouette, the sound of rumbling male voices around the corner of the house lured her outside to join them.

"So you got to meet Samantha." Garrett motioned her closer to where they'd been inspecting the foundation. "Kind of puts a face on what you're trying to accomplish here, doesn't it?"

"It definitely does." She eyed Luke. "What brings you here?"

When she and Paris had met him on the street the other day, he'd wasted no time in turning down Garrett's invitation to join them at the house. So much for an opportunity to coax a smile from him. But now here he was.

He jerked his head in his cousin's direction. "Garrett wants to get some of the junk out of your way this morning."

A surge of hope shot through her at the prospect of that chore being done before youth group parents and kids toured the place that evening. "That would be wonderful."

Garrett nodded. "We figured it couldn't hurt to make it as presentable as we can."

We? That was doubtful knowing how Luke felt about the Masons. Apparently Garrett had a God-given gift for persuasion—either that or had something he could hold over Luke's head in the form of blackmail.

Nevertheless, depending on how quickly the two of them cleared things out, she might have time to vacuum and mop floors. Travis had probably put out the word about the condition of the place, but while no amount of preliminary effort would win a Good Housekeeping award, anything she could do to make it less scary to kids and their folks would be worth it.

She followed the two men back into the house where Luke secured the screen door wide open, then he and Garrett grabbed the ends of the sagging sofa.

Leave it to these guys not to clear a path to the door. She snatched up a box of knickknacks and set it to the side. "What can I do to help?"

"Just stay out of the way," Luke mumbled.

Garrett offered an apologetic grin. "He means so you don't get hurt. Men moving furniture can prove dangerous to innocent bystanders. Right, Luke?"

Luke grunted as he lifted his end of the sofa with an impressive display of muscle. "Yeah. Right."

Garrett winked at her as he heaved up his side

and stepped over a box of magazines. "Don't pay any attention to him. He got up on the wrong side of the bunk this morning."

She scurried to step out on the porch before they did, but close enough in case her assistance was needed as they maneuvered their way out. It wasn't.

The sofa was loaded without incident into the bed of Luke's pickup, then a decrepit coffee table, two end tables and an armchair losing its stuffing followed. Boxes full of miscellaneous items wedged neatly into crooks and crannies.

"That's it for this round." From where he stood, next to the truck's storage chest, Luke pulled out a handful of rubber tarp straps, then efficiently secured the load. "Ready to roll, Garrett?"

Garrett glanced at his watch. "I'm afraid if I ride along, I'll cut it too close to get back to conduct that funeral. Why don't you take Delaney?"

She cast a bewildered look at Luke, then Garrett. "Me? I can't lift that sofa."

Garrett shrugged. "You don't have to. Someone will help out on the other end. Ride along and keep an eye on the stuff in the back, make sure nothing comes loose. You can do that, can't you?"

"I suppose so."

"Don't worry about it, Delaney. I can manage." Luke briskly moved to the driver's side of the pickup and opened the door, obviously not wanting to waste time in a debate.

She shouldn't go along. There was more than enough to do here at the house to get ready for tonight. And yet…what harm would come of enjoying Luke's company for an hour or so?

For whatever reason, despite being dead set against helping the Masons, he'd taken time from his workday to help clean out the worst of the bulky stuff from downstairs. He didn't have to do that, and Garrett seemed to think it important that someone ride shotgun and keep an eye on things in the bed of the truck while Luke focused on the road.

"You'll lock up when you have to leave?" Pulling one of the house keys from her jeans pocket, she tossed it to Garrett who easily caught it midair.

"Can do."

"Well, then—" With a sense of anticipation she chose not to analyze, she jogged to the passenger-side door of the big truck, then peeped through the window to wave at a somewhat confused-looking Luke. "Let's roll."

Chapter Eight

He wasn't quite sure how this happened, but it didn't feel half bad to be driving through Hunter Ridge with a pretty lady seated beside him. Well, not beside him exactly. Rags had situated himself between them, hogging part of Delaney's seat and seeming to enjoy her arm looped around his neck.

"So where are we going with this stuff?"

"To a secondhand shop in Canyon Springs first. Then what he doesn't want we can let Goodwill take a look at, take anything that's recyclable to the recycle center and haul anything that's left to the landfill."

He lifted a hand to acknowledge Packy who'd stepped outside the Log Cabin Café to continue a chat with a customer. No doubt he'd get razzed about Delaney the next time he set foot inside for a cup of coffee.

"I met that guy when Paris and I had lunch there." Delaney turned inquisitive eyes on Luke. "Why do they call him Packy?"

"Packrat. His place makes Bachelor Bob's look like a showcase. Somebody should get one of those TV shows specializing in hoarding interventions to conduct an inspection."

She gave Rags a hug as they headed out of town. "Hunter Ridge has a lot of interesting people, doesn't it?"

"More than you can count, I imagine." Most small towns were probably like that. People couldn't easily hide their idiosyncrasies from neighbors the way they often could in the relative anonymity of cities.

"So your family founded the town, right?"

"Harrison 'Duke' Hunter, to be exact. My great-great-grandfather. He settled here in the early 1900s. Established a lodging place for hunters and backcountry explorers. Outdoorsmen—and -women—have been the core of Hunter Ridge ever since. Its life's blood."

"It seems that a growing art community is pumping in a fresh, life-sustaining supply, too."

Delaney gave them too much credit. Who knew what propaganda Sunshine had filled her head with?

"That population is relatively new and not likely one that the town can sustain indefinitely. It's not the heart and soul of Hunter Ridge and don't let anyone else tell you different."

"So how new is new?"

"Maybe five, six years, although it had its roots in a dispute that occurred thirty years ago." Thanks to his aunt—whom he remembered, although he'd been only a youngster at the time of her departure.

"Oooh, I love history. What happened?"

He applied the brake as they rounded another thickly forested curve. Delaney may as well know the whole story and come to understand that Hunter Ridge belonged to the Hunter family—and those who were like-minded. Not the newcomers.

"My Uncle Doug—one of Dad's brothers—and Uncle Doug's wife Charlotte divorced. She was a wealthy city gal who'd caught Uncle Doug's eye while away in college. Love at first sight and all that. It didn't take her long, though, to figure out she hated it here."

"Why? This area is beautiful." She gave Rags another hug, then stared out the window thoughtfully as they started down the twisting, tree-lined road that would eventually bottom out to a bridge over Hunter Creek, then climb to the next ridge and the main highway. It was a tough incline to get up or down come winter.

"Apparently she thought she was better than everyone else in town." He adjusted his rearview mirror. "So it wasn't long after their first child was born that she left with the kid and sicced a bunch of big city lawyers on Uncle Doug. She got custody of their son and a sweet chunk of his property, too. Property which she sat on for a lot of years, paying the taxes but letting it stand vacant.

And become an eyesore and a constant reminder to the community of what she thinks of it."

"That's mean."

"Yeah, it was." He could remember as a teen peering into the empty storefronts, hearing his parents and grandparents grumble about Aunt Char's vindictiveness. "But maybe half a dozen years ago, she started leasing and selling off pieces of property to those she knew would most irritate townspeople."

Delaney's mouth took a downturn. "Artists?"

He nodded. "And not just any artists, but the more free-spirited, nonconformist variety."

Boy, did Aunt Char know how to pick 'em.

"However—" He slowed as they crossed the bridge stretching over the creek, the water level diminishing now that the winter snow runoff had mostly flowed downstream. "The upside is that Hunter Enterprises was born. The extended family pulled together to protect remaining properties inherited from our ancestor."

Delaney didn't respond. Did she not care for his take on the artistic types that were invading the community? He increased pressure on the gas pedal as they started up the incline on the other side of the creek and Delaney turned to look at their cargo.

He glanced in his rearview mirror when she didn't immediately settle back into her seat. "Everything okay back there?"

"Looks to be. You secured it well. I was noticing how beautiful it is looking up at the ridge behind us. The sky is so blue above the treetops."

"Yeah, it's amazing country. But then you'd already know that, having lived in Canyon Springs."

Delaney turned again to face the windshield, then squared her shoulders as if something had been weighing on her mind. "I get the impression, Luke, that you think my wanting to help the Masons is a mark against my own values and beliefs." She placed a hand on his forearm. "That's not true at all."

He drew a breath as her hand warmed his skin, trying to refocus on the road. "I don't—"

"But you think I'm wrong, and I know deep down you hope that tonight the other parents and kids will reject the project. But you're helping today because you want to make it look as if it doesn't matter to you."

"Why would I do that?"

She withdrew her hand, her gaze still intent. "I don't know."

He didn't know, either. When Garrett called to see about bringing his truck over, saying no had been his first instinct. With Garrett's and the women's ministries buy-in, it was pretty much a done deal. What did it matter if the junk was cleaned out or not? It wasn't as if she'd be hosting an open house this evening.

As they topped the winding road where it

joined the highway, Luke checked for traffic, then pulled out.

He didn't exactly know why he'd agreed to help today. But one thing was for certain. It had nothing to do with the sweet-smelling, golden-haired beauty sitting here beside him, her searching gaze all but boring a hole through him.

No, sir. Not a thing.

Luke Hunter is one stubborn man.

She'd repeated that mantra to herself all the way to Canyon Springs and back even though they'd kept the remainder of their limited conversation to superficialities rather than the Masons and the project house.

She'd spent most of the return drive looking out the window as the endless stands of ponderosa pine flashed by, trying to ignore the masculine presence behind the wheel. Repeatedly she reprimanded herself for trying to get him to understand that although she supported the work on the Mason house, that didn't mean that she necessarily agreed with their lifestyle.

And now, watching him tonight across the room of the project house, arms folded and deep in discussion with two sets of youth group parents, she couldn't forget how he'd laughed when he'd first stepped through the door. For a reason lost to her, the fairy lights strung across the top of the now-curtainless drapery rods and the appetizers and punch bowl arranged on a tablecloth-covered card table amused him.

Did he think she'd usher people into a cold dark house?

But the ninety-minute open house was almost over and Garrett, his little cousin Chloe clinging to his hand, had confided he thought all was going well, that their efforts to declutter had paid off. Of course, that left plenty of projects that still needed attention. An overgrown yard. Worn carpeting. Peeling wallpaper. Scarred woodwork. A kitchen in desperate need of emergency triage.

And the infamous half bath.

Upstairs Bachelor Bob boxes of items unwanted by his family had been shoved against the walls of the bedrooms to allow for a tour. Luke had agreed before he'd returned to work that afternoon to get them moved out at the first opportunity. But even if parents gave the project a thumbs-up tonight, the kids *wouldn't* be starting tomorrow. At least not inside.

Thanks to Travis and Anna's father.

"I'm thankful Luke Hunter knows something about flooring in old houses," Min Chambers confided as Delaney ladled a cup of punch and handed it to her, her whispered comment not quite echoing Delaney's take on the situation. "Checking out the under-layers of the linoleum in the kitchen for asbestos somehow escaped our checklist."

Yes, leave it to Luke to think of that. Nevertheless… "I agree. Quite thankful."

"Don't you worry." Min nodded warmly in Luke's direction. "This will get taken care of and, thanks to him, no harm will come to anyone."

Min slipped her arm around Delaney's waist for a quick hug, then moved off to mingle with the remaining few parents and teens to answer questions. Travis hadn't put in an appearance tonight and Anna stayed only a short while with Sybil, asking probing questions about the estimated cost of supplies and labor should the project be outsourced to others rather than completed by the youth group.

Suddenly tired, Delaney headed to the kitchen where Luke had blocked the entrance with a kid gate to prevent anyone from entering the possibly contaminated area where Delaney had already pulled up a sizeable section of the linoleum. A harsh overhead light more than revealed the room's shortcomings, including the telltale, plastic-covered section of flooring by the back door. She'd been so sure of this project, excited from the moment she'd first met with Min and Lois about the opportunity to take part. Certain of God's leading.

And now this.

It wasn't that she didn't want the space to be safe for the youth group to work in or for the Masons. She did. But why couldn't Luke have thought of that potential problem earlier in the week when there might have been time to get it taken care of? Surely he hadn't intentionally withheld his speculation until today, had he?

But it was only after their return from Canyon Springs that he'd pointed out a section of flooring where she'd tried to pull up the layers, hoping to find wooden floor beneath. Cautioning her about the prevalence of asbestos in older linoleum, he'd wet paper towels and placed them over the area, then covered it with heavy-duty garbage bags, as well.

"Staring at it won't make it go away."

At the sound of Luke's voice, she drew her gaze away from the plastic blanketing the surface by the back door. This delay forfeited any momentum generated by the few kids who shared her vision for the place and were most enthusiastic about getting started.

"I know you're not happy with me right now, Delaney."

There was no point in denying that. "What if the flooring does contain asbestos?"

"Then it will be removed."

"But doesn't that take time we don't have? Won't the kitchen have to be sealed off and men in hazmat suits come in to remove it?"

"Could be. But look, the odds are that it will be free of asbestos. Just the same, I had to bring the possibility to your and Min's attention."

"I know." She leaned back against the doorway. "I'm glad you did. Really. It's just that—"

"I know we don't see eye to eye on this project." He stepped closer to look down at her. "But I'm not trying to throw a wrench into your plans. I only—"

Her breath caught. He had such amazing eyes.

"I only—" he repeated as though something had distracted him "—am looking out for everyone. I—"

"Daddy? Can we go home now?"

They turned as Chloe came up behind them, looking as sleepy as Delaney was beginning to feel. Eight o'clock at night was nearing an eight-year-old's bedtime. Her own wasn't far off. It had been a long day.

"Ready to head out?" Luke lifted her into his arms and she cuddled against him, but her attention focused on Delaney.

"I like your hair," Chloe said softly.

Delaney smiled and self-consciously fluffed her unruly mane. As windy as it had been today, she must look a fright. "Thank you."

"Anna likes it, too."

"Then tell Anna thank you, as well."

"I don't know if Travis likes it. I'll ask him." Chloe pulled back slightly to look her father in the eye. "Do you like her hair, Daddy? She looks like a princess in a book, doesn't she?"

He glanced at Delaney, studying her almost as

if seeing her for the first time. Her clothes. Her hair. Delaney's cheeks warmed when their gazes met. And held.

He abruptly looked away to brush back his daughter's bangs. "Yes, she does look like a princess, Chloe."

Poor Luke, bullied into that admission.

He shifted the child in his arms and she looped her own around his neck to settle in once more. Safe. Secure. Knowing she was welcomed and loved.

Luke nodded to the floor. "Like I said earlier, I have a friend in Phoenix who knows people who do this kind of testing. I'll see if we can get it expedited."

"Thanks." But it would be too late for weekend work in the kitchen. She'd hoped to get started on stripping wallpaper, cleaning out drawers and cabinets and, of course, pulling up that ugly linoleum. "I guess we wait, then, to see who shows up tomorrow. And hope they bring their rakes and gloves."

Would Luke assure her that Anna and maybe even Travis would be there to help? That he might be there, too?

He didn't.

Why was she hoping he'd join them? The beauty of a group project like this was that it created an atmosphere conducive to teamwork and casual conversation that often evolved into deeper discussions. Discussions teens might not indulge in if mom or dad were present.

Chloe's eyes were growing heavier by the minute. Luke noticed, too.

"Say good-night to Delaney."

The girl waved. "Good night, Delaney."

Luke nodded in Delaney's direction as well, then the three of them returned to the now-empty living room where a good-hearted soul had already whisked away the punch bowl, candles and any remaining appetizers. Min, no doubt, bless her heart.

Luke paused, his voice echoing slightly in the room now devoid of furniture and draperies. "Why don't you lock up and I'll see you to your car?"

"Thanks, but you don't need to do that. I'll be fine. It's not even completely dark yet."

"It will be shortly. This may be a small town, Delaney, but the world is changing. And, unfortunately, not all for the better. Chloe and I'll see you to your car, then follow you to your place. Make sure you get inside safely."

From the look in his eyes, one that she'd seen leveled on Travis, there would be no point in debating the issue.

"Okay. Thanks." Why did she suddenly feel safe? Protected. Dwayne was a good man in many ways, but he'd never seen her to her car. Never saw her home after she left his place or even had her call when she got home safely.

It was nice for a change to know someone cared.

No, not *cared*. But Luke was concerned. Cautious. Felt responsible. Probably not much different than how he felt for the welfare of his kids... or any stranger.

Why did that conclusion not make her day?

Chapter Nine

"If you're going to follow her home like a pitiful lost pup, you should at least ask her out."

Luke's younger brother Grady eyed him as the two of them flipped over another of the heavy benches and placed it, seat-side down, on top of an oak-slabbed table. They'd worked in unison from one end of the Hunter's Hideaway dining room to the other, almost without thinking, having done this nightly for most of their lives to make for easier cleaning under tables. That is, of course, except for the dozen years before Luke—the prodigal, his brother called him—had returned home.

While he hadn't been turned away at the door and Mom and Grandma Jo were beside themselves with joy at his return, it wasn't as if Dad had prepared a fatted calf on his behalf. Grady, who hadn't turned his back on Hunter's Hideaway, was still his father's golden boy. Now his brother was poking his nose in where it didn't belong and thought he should ask Delaney on a date? Fat chance.

"Butt out."

Grady grinned, his lopsided smile and sturdy build reminding Luke of photos he'd seen of Grandpa Hunter in his younger days.

"Ask who out?" their little sister Rio called from the far side of the empty room where she was wiping down one of the booth tables. *Little* sister, of course was relative, considering she'd be twenty-one years old next spring and had been turning male heads since she was sixteen. Ever since Luke's timely return to Hunter Ridge, he and Grady had been keeping those they believed to be unworthy suitors at a distance. Which wasn't always something Rio appreciated.

But a brother had to do what a brother had to do, right?

Luke gave Grady a warning look as Rio approached with a curious light in her eyes. Dressed in her usual workday attire—boot-cut jeans, a too-well-fitted chambray shirt and Western boots—her layered, flaxen hair cascaded down her back. A tough little gal who saw to the welfare of the Hunter horses, she wasn't much interested in froufrou. And thus was Anna's idol.

"Ask who out?" she repeated, sidling up to Grady where they both fixed their gazes on their oldest brother.

"That cute youth group worker who's leasing Charlie and Emma's old place for the summer. He followed her home this evening."

Rio's eyes warmed. "You did, Luke?"

"No, I didn't. I—" But he had. Technically, anyway.

"Yeah, he did." Grady nodded in his direction.

"Oh, *really*?" Rio clucked her tongue thoughtfully.

"When I was coming home tonight," Grady continued, "I saw Luke sitting out in his truck in front of her place while she unlocked the door, then waved goodbye."

"Poor boy," Rio taunted. "She didn't invite you in for a cup of java? A good-night kiss?"

"If he doesn't ask her out soon, the reputation of the Hunter males will be shot." Grady, who played the field himself, shook his head, a mournful look in his eyes. "We're not known for doing pitiful."

Luke huffed a breath. "I saw her safely home from Bachelor Bob's place after the youth group parents met there. That's all I was doing. I had Chloe with me."

"Ah." Rio exchanged a meaningful look with Grady. "Chloe, his resident chaperone."

Grady punched him playfully in the shoulder. "You're going to have to keep that kid at home if you intend to make time with the ladies."

"I don't know about that." His sister studied Luke openly. "Good-looking single man. Cute kid. Even has a trusty sidekick in that mutt of his. A combo like that might melt a few female hearts."

Luke wagged his finger at them, fighting an exasperated smile. "Look, you two—"

"What's all the fuss about?" Eighty-year-old Grandma Jo drew their attention to the open doorway leading from the inn's lobby. Surveying them almost regally, she placed her hands at the waist of her jeans. Luke couldn't imagine his grandmother wearing anything else during the warmer months of the year. Denim and a collared shirt in the summer and wool slacks and a turtleneck sweater in the winter. Hair upswept and secured with combs year-round. The only time in his whole life that he'd seen her in a dress was at a wedding or funeral.

Grady grasped Luke by the shoulder. "We're giving our big brother here a hard time."

Just like old times. Occasionally they'd comfortably lapse into that big-bro-little-bro dynamic like they'd done this evening. But too often since Luke's return it was awkwardly apparent that despite their birth order, Grady was their father's right-hand man. The go-to guy. The one who would be running Hunter's Hideaway when—if ever—Dad stepped down from that demanding role.

It galled, but Luke had only himself to blame.

"We think," Rio filled in, "that Luke needs to start dating again. Grady believes he's found the right woman. All he's lacking is your approval."

Luke snorted. Everybody knew that after the

disastrous business between Uncle Doug and Aunt Char their grandmother claimed the right to vet any new additions to the family.

Grandma looked at Luke, who only shook his head, then to Grady. "And who might that woman be?"

"Delaney Marks. You've seen her at church. The summer youth volunteer."

"You have an interest in this young lady, Luke?"

He shot a threatening look at Grady.

"No, ma'am, I don't." That was the truth. Mostly. He was a man, after all. But would he follow through on any mutual attraction? Unequivocally, no. He owed it to his kids to put them first, not to forget the role he may have played in depriving them of a mother.

But his family didn't know about any of that and, God willing, none of them ever would.

"A shame," his grandmother pronounced, almost as if she would have given him the go-ahead to pursue Delaney. "May I speak with you a moment, Luke? In private?"

What was he in for now? A lecture from Grandma about the importance of carrying on the family name? Hadn't he already taken care of that with three kids? Following her from the room, he glared back at his brother who wasn't even attempting to suppress a smile. Rio's eyes danced with mischief.

He couldn't wait to leave for Kansas.

He trailed his grandmother into the open space that served as a lobby and registration area, then past the staircase leading to the second-floor guest rooms. Josephine Hunter had ruled the Hunter clan since Grandpa Hunter's passing fifteen years ago. Maybe even before that, if you considered her the power behind the throne. Her mind sharp, her attitude spunky, she carried herself with an astonishingly aristocratic bearing for a woman her age. Definitely someone to be respected, grandma or no grandma.

Together they entered a side parlor where she moved around to the far side of a mahogany desk and sat down in the chair behind it.

"Close the door, please. Then have a seat."

He obeyed, then lowered himself into a leather wingback chair, his legs outstretched. He glanced at his watch. Ten o'clock.

"I can't linger too long, Grandma. Chloe's tucked in for the night and I left Travis in charge, which sometimes doesn't set well with Anna." The teens were allowed to stay up later on a Friday night.

"This will only take a few minutes."

He might as well get this over with, but he'd already learned his lesson. He should have parked across the street in front of the Hunter Ridge office tonight, not in front of Delaney's place where Grady—or anyone else in town—could see him escorting her home. What was a man who'd been raised to be a gentleman to do? He couldn't leave her alone in that old house with night descending, could he?

"You can rest assured, Grandma, that I have no intentions of dating Delaney Marks."

His grandmother frowned. "What I want to talk to you about has nothing to do with that young lady."

What then? He sat up straighter in his chair, leaning slightly forward.

"Hunter Enterprises has been approached about offering a young man a part-time position, one that could potentially become permanent if it works out."

"Doing what?" It wasn't unusual to test-drive potential employees on a part-time basis, but why was she talking to him about it? Grady and Dad did the hiring and firing around here. Her oldest grandson was solely the resident bean counter— and one his father and brother didn't even trust enough to take his advice that they needed to upgrade their systems.

"Grady could use more help with maintenance work since Hernando retired. He'd hoped Miles could pick up the slack, but he's not a young man now either."

"Yeah, he's getting on up there." Like Hernando, Miles had been around since he himself had been a kid. "So, what does this have to do with me?"

Grandma stood and stepped behind her chair, hands resting on the back of it. "The candidate in question has a disadvantaged background, has made mistakes in his life."

"You're saying he has a criminal record? Is he an ex-con?" Depending on what his conviction was for, he wouldn't want him hanging around kids. Neither his nor those of their guests.

"No chronic criminal convictions. A first DUI."

Driving under the influence. Drugs or alcohol? There seemed to be more than enough of that these days. No one taking responsibility for themselves or for the safety of others.

"In that case," Luke concluded, "I think this is something better left to be decided by Dad and Grady. If they want to take responsibility for the guy, that's their business."

"The decision has already been made."

He frowned. "Then I guess I don't understand what you want from me."

"I want you to be aware of this because…" She drew a breath. "You've met the young man. Have even had a few unpleasant encounters with him in the past year. And with his oldest son."

A knot tightened in Luke's stomach as he gripped the arms of the chair. Young man? If she was talking about who he thought she was talking about, midthirties wasn't exactly what he'd call a *young* man. Then again, when you're eighty…

Luke rose to his feet. "You're hiring Benton Mason?"

"We are."

"Who talked you into that kind of—" He stopped himself before uttering the word *foolishness*. Grandma was anything but foolish and wouldn't take kindly to that label.

"He's a veteran, Luke," she said quietly. "Did you know that?"

"Veteran of what?"

"Ex-army." Her hands tightened on the back of the chair.

Luke stared. That irresponsible artist was an army vet? "No way."

"Iraq and Afghanistan."

Why hadn't anyone around here heard about that? Everyone in town knew Luke had been overseas in the thick of combat. Yet upon meeting Benton, there had been no attempt on his part to bond with a fellow veteran. No attempt to discover if they had any friends in common or to draw mutual support.

Luke grimaced. "Dishonorably discharged, then?"

Grandma shook her head. "Honorably."

"He told you that?"

"Your father has seen the discharge papers.

High Country Hope Ministries vouches for him. He and his wife have been separated since Christmas last year, although not legally. You already know about the drunk driving incident and that Hope Ministries is fixing up a place for them to rent when he comes home to his family."

"So Hunter's Hideaway is supposed to foot the bill for this do-gooder experiment?"

"He'll earn his keep."

This risky move wouldn't have been his choice, vet or no vet. But no one had asked his opinion. Even now, Grandma wasn't looking for his blessing, merely informing him.

"When's he start?"

"August. As soon as the house is finished and he can move back in with his family."

With a shake of his head, Luke fisted his hands on his hips.

Grandma Jo stepped from around the chair. "I wanted you to know in advance, Luke, because I know you aren't fond of him or his wife."

"Or that annoying kid of theirs who's caused Anna such grief."

Her lips tightened. "I didn't want there to be any surprises."

A little late for that.

First Delaney, now Grandma. Was he the only person on the planet who thought Benton could only spell trouble?

* * *

Thank You, Lord. Watching the activity surrounding her on Saturday at the Mason house, Delaney gave a happy sigh of relief. They had a good turnout this morning. Showing parents and kids around the place last night hadn't dissuaded many from signing on for the project—nor had the news that the house was for the family of Benton Mason.

So Luke had been wrong—or at least partially so. Only two parents had declined to allow their teens to participate when the name Mason had come up. She couldn't help feeling a tiny sense of satisfaction in that. Would Luke's concerns ease up now that he saw a handful of parents here today willing to pitch in? Would he recognize that her judgment wasn't entirely off-base?

She scooped up another rake full of dried brown pine needles and emptied them into a thirty-nine-gallon yard bag anchored in a metal stand. Similar stands dotted the entire yard surrounding the house as teens and a scattering of parents teamed up to rake pine needles into two-foot-high "haystacks" ready for bagging.

She glanced over at Anna who, with Chloe's help, dragged an oversize garbage bag from place to place, gathering hundreds of pristine, sun-dried pinecones the size of an adult's fist.

"How's it going, Anna? Counting your pennies already?"

Crafters, as Delaney knew, used pinecones for wreath making and tree decorations. A net bag holding six or seven cones often sold for five dollars at national craft stores, so Anna figured she could easily undercut that price or quadruple the bag size and make a tidy profit from local and regional crafters.

Anna grinned at her. "I am. Ka-ching!"

Luke had quite the entrepreneur on his hands.

"Me, too," Chloe chimed in as she examined a pinecone, trying to determine if it was a keeper.

Travis had showed up, too, and he and Kendrick were using a pole saw to manually trim dead "ladders" from a cluster of young pines while Nelson and another boy cleaned out rotting leaves and deadwood from surrounding bushes. Up by the porch steps, Sybil and Scottie had finished filling a half barrel with soil, flats of pink-and-white petunias at their feet awaiting transplant.

But best of all, Luke himself stood on a ladder, cleaning fistfuls of decaying pine needles from the gutters and dropping them to the ground where a teenager below swiftly bagged them.

Why did his presence make her so happy? Much to her embarrassment, Paris had been quick to pick up on that last week. Oh, sure, he was a good-looking, physically fit guy. But Dwayne had been all that, too. And nobody complained about it being a hardship to gaze upon Pastor McCrae as he shared God's word from the pulpit, but her heart didn't do a tap dance whenever he appeared. So it was more than that.

Maybe it was the fact that Luke's eyes sometimes held a sadness that she longed to chase away. Or that it was evident he loved his kids more than life itself. Or maybe it had something to do with the fact that he'd made sure she got home safely last night. He didn't have to do that. These days many men didn't even offer.

"Yo, Dad!" Travis called. "Can I borrow your truck keys? It's time to pick up the pizza you promised."

So Luke had lured him here with pizza?

She watched as Luke descended the ladder, handed over the keys and counted bills into the open palm of his son. More money than a single pizza would cost.

"Stick around, everybody!" Travis waved the cash in the air as he and Kendrick trotted toward the truck. "Pizza is on its way."

A rousing cheer went up from the kids, but she didn't like the sound of that one bit. Had Luke *bribed* all the teenagers to show up with a promise of pizza?

Luke headed back to the ladder, but she beelined across the yard to cut him off before he could climb up.

"Luke."

"What's up?"

"Can I speak with you a minute? In private?"

He glanced around the yard as the others settled back into their work. "I guess so. Sure."

She motioned to him and he followed her to the backyard where, as they rounded the corner of the house, he raised a hand to get the attention of those working there. "They've gone to get the pizza."

"All right!" Fist-pumps and whistles accompanied the announcement.

So he *had* bribed them. But why? He didn't even think this project was a good idea.

He turned to her. "So what did you need to see me about?"

She didn't want to talk in front of the kids, so motioned for him to again follow, this time behind the freestanding garage where she halted. "Did you get these kids to show up here with a promise of pizza?"

He shrugged. "Worked, didn't it? I watch my money closely, but pizza for a dozen kids didn't break the bank. So don't worry about it."

He thought she was concerned about his financial situation? She let out an exasperated breath. "What I mean is, it's one thing to reward them for a job well done once it's, well, *done.*"

"Kids are kids. They get hungry."

"But the whole point in this kind of project is

to help young people learn that it's about giving, not getting. You know, more blessed to give than receive? It would have been one thing if you'd shown up with pizza and surprised them all—but quite obviously they knew beforehand that pizza was coming."

"What's the big deal?"

"I told you—"

"I motivated them, Delaney. It's as simple as that. You were there Sunday night and saw the re-action the teens had to the Masons, to their oldest boy. And on Tuesday you couldn't have missed the mixed responses to this place. Pizza gave the borderline kids a nudge."

She shook her head. He didn't get it.

"Come on. You're acting as though I'm lur-ing them into a drug ring or something. This is a church project. One which, I'll remind you, you initiated." A flicker of confusion flashed briefly in his eyes. "I thought you'd be pleased that so many kids showed up."

He did this for her?

In her dreams, maybe. There was no point, though, in arguing. What was done was done. Unfortunately, he'd set the tone for future project days. Would the kids expect someone to foot the bill for pizza all the time now?

Before she could decide on an appropriate re-sponse, Luke angled a glance at her, looking as he probably had as a boy when trying to get out of a punishment.

"So I don't get as much as a thank-you?"

Boy, had he botched that. But she was being unreasonable. Too idealistic.

She wasn't, however, a parent raising two teens like he was, so he needed to keep that in mind. As a single, childless woman who didn't have a whole lot of life experience, her knowledge of parenting would be limited to women's magazines or a psychology class she'd taken in college. None of which prepared anyone—man *or* woman—for reality, including the occasional need for a healthy dose of, yes, bribery.

He wasn't quite sure, though, why he'd sprung for pizza and had Travis and Anna put out the word. It would have been altogether better had the turnout been lousy enough to send Delaney, Garrett and Lois back to the drawing board to rethink things. To find a better project. Vet or no vet, anything involving Benton and Lizzie Mason was dubious.

Her brow now wrinkled in thought, Delaney looked torn as to how to respond to his searching query for a word of thanks. Or would Grady label it as pitiful? As fishing for a compliment from a pretty woman? But obviously a thank-you wasn't going to come without a struggle.

"I don't mean to sound ungrateful, Luke. But

I believe it's important that young people learn to give freely, not always look at what's in it for them."

"Agreed." He nodded, relieved that they could come to a consensus. He was willing to take ownership of his actions. "Since you're heading up the project, I should have asked you beforehand. So I owe you an apology."

But he'd wanted a great turnout to be a surprise. Why? So he could show off his generosity? His thoughtfulness? Win her admiration? Compete with Garrett? He had no business doing that.

But taking the razzing from his brother and sister about Delaney last night...well, it had, oddly enough, felt kind of good. Good to be seen as someone still in the game. Not a loser relegated to the bench. They'd actually thought Delaney might be a romantic prospect for their older brother. Not that she was or ever would be. But yeah, it had felt good, and doing something nice for her today had felt even better.

Until she'd had a problem with it.

"I owe you an apology, too." Her eyes reflected her sincerity. "For accusing you of manipulating the kids."

He shrugged. "I guess I did precisely that, though."

"Yes, you did." A dimple surfaced in her cheek. "But thank you anyway."

He raised a doubtful brow.

"I mean it, Luke. Thank you. After refueling with pizza, maybe the kids will stick around a while longer and we can finish this first phase of the outdoor work today."

"That's entirely possible." But they'd have to do it without him. He'd promised his grandmother he'd be back to the Hideaway after lunch to put up new curtain rods in her suite. Dad and Grady both hated doing that kind of stuff, but for some reason he wished now he hadn't made that commitment.

"We have the framework for vegetable gardens to build next weekend," Delaney continued, her eyes bright, "and we need to plant veggies and more flowers. There are stepping-stones and cement benches to place, too, both of which were donated. But if we finish cleaning out the undergrowth and the pine needles today, we can move on from here next weekend."

"Sounds like a plan."

"Everything works for the good, right?" Her mood had lightened considerably now that she was focusing once again on the bright side. "Even the asbestos scare has us out here working while the weather's nice."

"Which reminds me..." Luke motioned toward the house. "That friend I told you about in Phoenix put me in touch with a guy who will be here on Thursday to cut out a section of the flooring in the kitchen. The bathrooms and entryway, too. He'll send them off for analysis."

Her brows tented. "Not until Thursday?"

"Earliest they can get here."

"And it could be widespread? Not just the kitchen?"

"Possibly. Most likely none of it's contaminated. But it'll get checked out and then we'll do whatever has to be done."

Why'd he say *we*, as if he and Delaney were teaming up on this? He'd better watch himself. She already had stars in her eyes too often when she looked at him. Not a good thing, as Marsha would certainly attest were she still alive to voice an opinion. If she had to do it over again, would she marry him—or show him the door?

Smacked by reality, he stepped back, realizing that without thinking he'd moved closer to Delaney as they'd talked. Even when being gently chastised, he'd been drawn to her. Literally.

"So," he said, forcing cheerfulness into his tone. "Let's get a piece of that pizza while there's still some left."

Chapter Ten

"It's been good talking to you, Delaney. I'm glad to hear your youth group project is coming along."

It was hard to tell, but over the phone Aunt Jen sounded more tired than when Delaney had picked her up for church the previous weekend and taken her out to lunch. But, as always, she'd insisted she was fine—and urged her niece to step up her job search. Delaney, however, had no intention of going anywhere until the project was completed. And, of course, not until sufficiently reassured that her aunt wouldn't need her.

"We're making good headway despite that storm that hit us last weekend." To her disappointment, it had been a soaker and they'd had to cancel the whole workday because the Hope Ministries board decided it was unwise for the young people to work indoors until the asbestos question was resolved.

"The roofers have been busy this past week. And a local contractor donated some insulated windows, so installation is taking place, as well.

Talk about an answered prayer. Several of the house's windows are in bad shape, and you know how the winter wind can creep in around the tiniest of crevices."

"I certainly do."

Not wanting to get in the way of the hired workers when the sun finally came out, Delaney had borrowed her aunt's sewing machine and spent most weekdays with a group of church ladies as they set out to accessorize the house. Curtains, throw pillows, wall hangings. She steered clear of the property except to drive by and see how things were progressing. But when the teens finished with the outdoor labor today, would the asbestos testing prove to be negative so they could start working on the interior next weekend? That would be Independence Day weekend, though. Would anyone show up?

The summer was already flying by too fast and the work she'd committed to stretched far beyond her original perception. Had she, as Luke had suggested, bitten off more than she and the youth group could chew?

Gripping her cell phone, she moved to the perimeter of the backyard, away from the noisy, rambunctious boys who'd taken a break from constructing three raised vegetable beds in a sunny patch of the yard for a quick game of touch football. They'd had another good Saturday workday turnout, a couple of parents leaving only a few minutes ago. But although Luke had dropped off Anna and Travis earlier in the day, he'd yet to put in an appearance.

She hadn't talked to him since a brief chat the day they'd shared "bribery" pizza with the teens. Not inclined to talk much about himself, she did manage to gain a glimpse into his military background and peek into what life must be like at Hunter's Hideaway, where he and his children lived near several family members.

She and her aunt visited a few more minutes before ending their conversation. Then she looked up just as Luke strode around the corner of the house, his trusty canine Rags at his heels. Her heart cheered at the sight of him and she watched in astonishment as he suddenly dashed into the thick of the football game and snagged a pass intended for Kendrick.

But before he could make a move, the pack of boys forgot that this was a touch game and tackled him.

With no layers of pine needles to cushion his fall, Luke hit the ground hard. Delaney cringed. But to her relief, he laughed as he sat up and handed off the ball to a grinning Kendrick. Rags checked him out to be sure he was okay, then Travis gripped his hand to help him to his feet.

"Serves you right, Dad."

Still laughing, Luke dusted himself off as

Kendrick tossed the ball high into the air, then caught it.

"Are you going to join us for a game, *Mister* Hunter?"

He shook his head, his fingers kneading the shoulder he'd landed on. "I think I'll pass, thank you. But I couldn't resist when I saw that pigskin sailing right past my nose."

It was then that Luke saw her, a suddenly sheepish grin surfacing only long enough to ramp up her heart rate before it disappeared. He bid the boys a farewell as he and Rags made their way off the temporary playing field to where she stood.

"Are you okay? You took quite a hit."

He drew back, as if her words had wounded his pride. "Of course. No harm done."

She couldn't help but laugh. "Boys will be boys—at any age?"

His brows lowered slightly.

"Something like that." He looked back at the yard, then to her once again. "It appears they're ready to fill in the framework with topsoil that the landscaping company dumped out front just as I was pulling up. We can get that cleared out of the driveway before the workers return again on Monday."

"Things are moving along." Then, looking up at him, she giggled. "You have a horn."

"What?"

"A horn sticking up." Without thinking, she

stepped close and reached into his hair to snag a long pine needle. Her throat suddenly went dry as her fingertips made contact with the short, soft strands.

Startled eyes met hers but, nevertheless, she managed to triumphantly hold up the captured brown spike, longer than the length of her hand.

"See?" she said somewhat breathlessly as she gazed up at him, for a fleeting moment envisioning her younger self slipping the pine needle into the cedar keepsake chest she kept on top of her dresser.

Come on, Delaney, you're not fifteen anymore, crushing on the boy in math class.

Luke plucked the pine needle from her fingers, studied it for a moment, then tossed it aside.

So much for mementos.

"Thanks for the rescue." He took a step back as if to put some distance between them, then brushed his hand roughly through his hair to dislodge any other foreign objects caught there when he'd hit the ground. "My kids get their kicks from a good laugh at my expense. Dad with a horn sticking out of the top of his head would certainly make their day."

Delaney stifled another giggle. "Sorry."

A smile twitched. "Like I said, I'm used to being teased by my kids."

"Now, now, they only tease you because they *love* you." Her breath caught again, hoping he didn't think she was implying…well, anything about her own motive for teasing him.

He held her gaze for a long moment, the emotion in his eyes shifting at lightning speed from surprise to curiosity to open male interest, then shuttering back to that resigned sadness she'd too often seen reflected there.

Think of something to say that will make him happy again.

"Where's that adorable Chloe today?"

"With her grandma." He nodded toward the football game still in progress. "I guess we'd better get these guys hauling topsoil before they think they're done for the day."

But as he walked away, she couldn't help but visually search the ground for the lone pine needle she'd plucked from the soft strands of Luke's hair.

As Luke strode across the backyard, he slapped his hands together in a loud clap and Rags leaped to his feet. "Come on, boys. Back to business."

His heart pounding like a marching band drum, his thoughts were anywhere but on hauling dirt. Delaney had caught him off guard when her fingers had innocently slipped into his hair in search of the errant pine needle, sending a tremor down his spine that he prayed she hadn't felt.

Man, he must be losing it.

The boys joined the girls around front, pausing to inspect the perennials they'd planted along the perimeters of the porch. Blanket flower. Bee balm. Coreopsis. Bellflower. A few others he didn't recognize from helping in Grandma Jo's garden when growing up. The place was starting to shape up nicely, far more than he would have guessed when he'd originally invited himself along with Delaney for an inspection.

Delaney.

What was wrong with him? She was every bit as close to Travis's age as she was to his. Could he get arrested for having thoughts like wanting to catch her hand in his and pull her close for a kiss?

For crying out loud, they hardly knew each other.

He took a ragged breath and grabbed a shovel. "Travis. Kendrick. Bring those two wheelbarrows over here and let's get started."

The boys exchanged a glance at the firmness of his tone. A tone he hadn't much used since he'd left the military and stopped barking orders at subordinates. In unison, they snapped to attention and saluted. "Yes, sir! Right away, sir!"

But he didn't crack a smile. He had to get this dirt hauled out of the driveway and hauled out now. Then get himself out of there before he made a fool of himself.

For whatever reason, Luke was no longer in a good mood, the playfulness he'd exhibited during the touch football game having evaporated into thin air once he set to work. When she ventured to bring him a bottle of water, he paused only long enough to wipe the sweat from his forehead, down the water and hand the bottle back to her with a brisk nod and a polite thank-you.

Should she not have laughed at him because he had a pine needle sticking out of his hair? She thought he'd found that amusing, prompting an unmistakable flicker of interest in his eyes that had set her heart racing. So maybe it was something else that was on his mind. Something that had nothing to do with her.

She wandered over to where the girls were still planting flowers in the soil they'd earlier dug up. Not an easy task since the ground was hard. With such a short growing season at this high elevation, they'd gone the route of starting with nursery plants rather than from scratch with seeds. Anna was now sharing a few tips for loosening the root-bound flowers from their plastic pots. Seemed she had a nose for numbers *and* a green thumb.

As she was about to join the girls, Delaney caught a glimpse of a boy leaning against a ponderosa pine just outside the front edge of the property. A teenager, in jeans, T-shirt and tennis shoes. She waved and, after a moment's hesitation, he lifted his hand, as well.

She didn't recognize him. Was he a member of the youth group who hadn't been able to join the project earlier? Maybe one of the kids whose parents had decided he shouldn't take part, but his curiosity had gotten the better of him?

Setting Luke's empty bottle on the steps, she headed in the boy's direction. He pushed away from the tree, his gaze wary as she approached. Did he think she was going to run him off?

"Hi. I'm Delaney."

She held out her hand and, after a moment, the dark-eyed, dark-haired boy took a step forward to shake it.

"Drake."

Up close, he looked to be about fifteen, slightly unkempt, with a voice in that awkward, changing adolescent male stage. His physique, likewise, was filling out, his shoulders broadening, a boy-man not yet comfortable in his own skin. But it was the expression in his eyes that struck her most. Caution mingling with hope.

"Good to meet you, Drake." She motioned back toward the activity at the house. "Have you come to help us today?"

He shook his head. "Just…looking."

"The youth group from Christ's Church is fixing the place up as a summer project. We could always use more muscle, if you feel like pitching in. It's fun."

He stuffed his hands into his front pockets. "I don't think so."

"If you're not into yard work, next weekend we hope to begin on indoor projects. General cleaning, stripping wallpaper, painting. It should be lots of fun, too."

His eyes brightened. "I like to paint."

She gave him an encouraging smile. "Fantastic. We'll have plenty of that to do. Once the wallpaper is stripped, every single room needs to be repainted. Do you think you might like to join us for that?"

Before he could answer, something caught his attention behind her and the light in his eyes dimmed. She looked back at the house where the girls were standing by the porch, clustered together, voices low and solemn eyes focused in the direction of Delaney and Drake.

Puzzled, she turned again to the boy—but he was already striding, head down, across the street.

"Drake!" But he either didn't hear her or chose not to.

She made her way across the yard to the girls, who had broken apart to return to their gardening. "Is something wrong?"

A grimacing Anna faced her. "That boy you were talking to?"

"Yes. Drake."

"Drake *Mason*. Benton and Lizzie Mason's son."

Scottie joined Anna, slipping her arm around her shoulder. "He picked on Anna last year."

"I didn't know." Delaney looked at Luke's daughter with concern. That nice boy with the gentle, hopeful eyes was a bully? "I'm sorry, but I'm afraid I invited him to join us next week."

Sybil stared. "Join us?"

"He said he likes to paint."

A male voice scoffed and she turned to Travis who'd come around the corner with an empty wheelbarrow. "He likes to paint, all right. Like in tagging."

Malicious graffiti? Is that why his eyes had brightened, finding humor in saying that because he knew she didn't know who he was?

Bewildered, Delaney looked around the circle of doubtful faces now gazing at her.

"If he's coming next week—" Anna's words came quietly, reluctantly. "I won't be here."

"Me, neither," several of the girls said in unison.

Travis shook his head, his eyes clearly communicating that Delaney's mistake was major. "It's bad enough to be fixing up a house for the Masons, but inviting Drake here so he can make my little sister miserable? You can count me out, too. Probably everybody."

They were abandoning ship?

Trying not to panic, she held up her hand. "Now hold on, gang—"

"Dad's not going to like this, either." Travis jerked his head in his father's direction. Luke, having no doubt overheard at least part of the conversation, had placed the shovel on the graveled driveway and was heading toward them, his eyes dark with disapproval.

Oh, great.

Suddenly a yelp of laughter pierced the air as Kendrick and Nelson, arms flailing, came pounding into the front yard, Nelson's best friend Marty in hot pursuit with a wildly spraying hose in his hands.

"Look out!" The boys charged into their midst, sending Travis, the screaming girls and Delaney scattering, but not before the hose had done its damage.

A grinning Marty spun to shoot the water once again in Kendrick and Nelson's direction and, before she could remind herself that she was no longer seventeen years old, Delaney dashed toward him with a roar that would have made her Scottish ancestors proud.

Startled, he whirled toward her, the water hitting her full-force. She gasped, halted, then with renewed determination charged on, heedless of her sopping hair and wringing-wet clothes. With a squeal of laughter, the other girls rallied to join her, as did the boys. They'd almost had the spewing hose wrestled away from Marty when an ear-piercing whistle split the air.

"That's enough!"

Startled, all activity halted as they turned eyes toward Luke, his expression grim as the hose gushed water on the ground at their feet.

"Turn that water off."

The kids exchanged a quick glance at the brook-no-argument command, then Marty dashed around the corner of the house. The water cut to a dribble.

Luke folded his arms. "I hope you're proud of yourselves."

The sopping wet teens again exchanged a look with Delaney and each other. Then broke out laughing.

"Think it's funny, do you?" From Luke's tone, he obviously didn't.

The bedraggled work crew looked at each other again. Anna stifled a giggle. Then Delaney bravely stepped out to halt in front of Anna and Travis's father.

"Come on, Luke," she coaxed with a smile, but noticed the front of his shirt had been more than slightly dampened in the melee. "The kids are having fun. That's all. Don't be such an old—"

His sharp, unsmiling gaze brought her up short.

"Old what? Fuddy-duddy?" He shook his head in apparent exasperation as he gazed down at her. "It appears someone needs to be one around here."

"Now, Luke…"

He broke eye contact and headed back to where he'd left his shovel. Then glanced back at the teens. "Come on kids, let's get the tools picked up. Time to go."

"Now, wait a minute." She hurried after him,

lowering her voice when she again reached his side. "If you're mad at me—"

"I'm not mad at you." He blinked, all innocence. "Maybe disappointed."

Ouch.

"I mean, look at you." His impersonal gaze raked her from the long, dripping hair to her waterlogged jeans to her wet, sandal-clad toes. "You're supposed to be the adult here. Overseeing the project and setting an example. Seeing that no horseplay gets out of hand and no one gets hurt."

"Nobody's hurt."

"They could have been."

Why was he angry? "We were having fun, Luke. Don't take it out on the kids."

"I'm not taking anything out on the kids. It's almost noon and I'm sure they have chores to do at home or paying jobs they need to get to. And—" He gave her a pointed look. "I didn't spring for pizza today."

She placed her hand lightly on his forearm, her voice soft as she looked up to him in appeal. "Please, Luke."

Expressionless, he stared down at her. "And another thing, you and I will be having a talk about that Mason kid's participation."

He intended to shut out the boy this place was being fixed up for? Support the church youth in their boycott of the project?

Her stomach did a queasy rollover. "Luke—"

She tightened her grip on his forearm, but he pulled away to look over the top of her head where the kids had quickly put the wheelbarrows up by the house, gathered their tools and were drifting toward their vehicles parked along the street. Then he motioned to Travis and Anna who stood silently off to the side of the porch.

"Let's go." The shovel still in one hand, he moved to slip his free arm protectively around his daughter as they walked toward his truck. Rags, tail wagging as usual, followed.

Delaney stared in disbelief at their departing backs, anger and heartache mingling in equal proportions. With great effort she held herself back from dashing after them to demand that her side of things be heard.

But what *was* her side? That she'd innocently invited a seemingly nice, lonely-looking boy to join the youth group in their labors? Had wanted to give him the opportunity to make friends? That the kids were having fun and she'd joined in? How was that any different than Luke leaping into the boys' touch football game?

What did I do that was so awful, Lord?

When the Hunter trio reached the truck, Luke stowed their tools in the bed. But before she got in the cab, Anna looked back at Delaney with an apologetic half smile, obviously not understanding any better than Delaney did what had just transpired.

Travis's expression was unusually thoughtful as he stood to the side watching his father settle himself inside the truck. Then shifting his pondering gaze to Delaney, the teen lifted a hand in a parting wave before climbing into the vehicle, as well.

Doors slammed with finality. The engine roared to life. Then the truck pulled away behind the last of the departing vehicles transporting other teens. Delaney stood alone in the puddled yard, only an empty water bottle and a few unplanted flowers next to the porch to keep her company.

She fisted her hands at her sides, determined not to cry.

Something had gotten into Luke Hunter today. Something that amounted to more than her well-intentioned invitation to the Mason boy and the laughter-filled drenching. And, if Travis's unusually contemplative expression held a clue, it appeared Luke's son might know what it was.

Chapter Eleven

He'd overreacted. Big-time.

The kids had ridden home with him in silence as they stared out the window, their only communication a shake of their heads when he'd offered to pick up burgers and fries for lunch. He'd been rewarded with no more enthusiasm when he threw in a milk shake.

Now, on the following Saturday morning—Fourth of July weekend—he sat in his pickup, staring at the project house. With a new roof and a number of new windows, the yard neatly groomed and flowers brightening the border of the porch, even without a fresh coat of paint it looked like a whole different place than it had a few weeks ago.

Delaney's was the sole car parked on the street in front of him. He'd left a message on her phone yesterday morning that testing had confirmed the house was free of asbestos contamination. She hadn't returned the call, but he still needed to talk to her.

Figuring the Mason kid would be a no-show, he could have insisted that Anna and Travis come this morning, but Anna had already volunteered to help Rio and their cousin J.C. accompany several parties of horseback riders on trail rides. Travis, too, had committed to assisting his uncle Grady repair one of the wagons that would be used for a hay ride under the stars tomorrow evening. Hunter's Hideaway wouldn't be putting on a fireworks show, but at this altitude visitors would see a spectacular display of God's handiwork.

The dashboard clock confirmed it was already nine o'clock. Two hours later than the previous workday start times. But even if kids weren't boycotting the project due to Delaney's invitation to Drake, it was likely the turnout would be slim on a holiday weekend. Nevertheless, he needed to get his feet moving in the direction of the house so he could talk to Delaney alone.

He opened the truck door, then paused to glance at Rags who tilted his head curiously. "What am I going to say to her, buddy?"

That he couldn't stop thinking about her? How she made him feel alive in a way he hadn't felt in years? That her smiling presence and gentle fingers plucking the pine needle from his hair had unnerved him?

Or the added unfortunate truth? That a laughing, sopping-wet Delaney attempting to wrestle the hose from Marty, didn't look much older than Scottie, Anna and Sybil.

He stepped out of the vehicle and his dog leaped

to the ground. "She looked and acted like one of the kids."

Her mentioning that boys will be boys had uncomfortably reminded him of Packy's warning to keep an eye on Travis. And her calling to his attention that he was an old fuddy-duddy drilled home what he'd known from the moment he'd met her. She was young. Too young for him. And he'd immaturely taken that out on her and the kids.

Rags raced ahead and Luke reluctantly followed, then opened the screen door when he reached the house. The wooden interior door stood open and he stuck his head inside. The living room beyond the entry was empty. "Anybody home?"

After a long moment when he thought Delaney must be in the backyard, her voice carried from somewhere in the far reaches of the house. "I'm back here. In the kitchen."

Letting the screen door close behind him, he passed through the living and dining rooms, then paused in the doorway to the kitchen. Hair tied back and on her hands and knees, Delaney was prying up linoleum with a crowbar. In fact, she'd made considerable headway, so she must have been here for some time. Or maybe yesterday, too, after having gotten his message about the asbestos testing results.

"Good morning."

Brushing back a stray strand of hair, she didn't look up. "Good morning to you, too."

"You're coming right along there."

"Yep."

"Could you use some help?"

She looked up then, and he could see the hurt confusion in her eyes. The hurt he'd put there by acting like such a jerk. "Thanks, but I'll have plenty of help when the kids get here."

"Anna won't be able to make it."

"And Travis?"

"He has chores to take care of at the Hideaway. I'm not sure how many others will come on a holiday weekend. Lots going on in the high country. Family stuff."

She nodded, then resolutely returned to her work. Feeling dismissed, Luke started to turn away, then caught himself. "We need to talk, Delaney."

With a sigh, she sat back and placed the crowbar on the floor. At least she didn't intend to clobber him with it.

"Luke, when I invited Drake to join us, I didn't even know he was a Mason. And I certainly didn't know he'd been picking on Anna."

"That's not what I'm here to talk about. Not entirely, anyway." He didn't like towering above her, so approached to reach out his hand. After a moment's hesitation, her expression flickering uncertainly, she placed her small, soft hand in his and he helped her to her feet.

She immediately slipped her hands into her back pockets, watchfully waiting for him to continue. But where should he start?

"I was out of line last weekend. It's a fact that my kids, once they finally started speaking to me again, let me know in no uncertain terms. I've already apologized to them, but now I want to apologize to you."

"Thank you." No gushing forth with reassurance that his misbehavior had been nothing. That he didn't need to apologize. Forget about the whole thing. No hard feelings.

"I don't have any excuses, Delaney. I embarrassed my kids. The other kids. I embarrassed you. And… I suspect I hurt your feelings."

"Yes, you did. I've racked my brain trying to figure out what I did that was so wrong, besides inviting Drake."

"That was an honest mistake. You had no way of knowing." He ran his hand roughly through his hair. "Drake won't come back. He doesn't want to work. He was nosing around, trying to stir things up."

"Maybe so. But if the other kids are boycotting as a show of solidarity for Anna, that means they haven't yet bought into the project, taken ownership. And that's my fault."

"My calling a halt to the fun last week and

putting a damper on the work that had been accomplished didn't help."

"No, it didn't." Questioning hazel eyes probed his. "Why *did* you do that, Luke?"

If ever a man looked uncomfortable when a reasonable question was posed, it was Luke Hunter at this very moment.

"I don't think anyone would have gotten hurt," Delaney continued. "Do you? Honestly?"

"I can't say what might or might not have happened." He leaned back against the kitchen counter, dodging a direct answer. "But I believe safe is better than sorry."

"I do, too. But have you never had a water balloon fight? Turned a hose on one of your cousins?"

He shifted. "I have."

"Was anyone hurt?"

"No overnight stays in the ER, if that's what you mean." A slight smile lifted the corner of his mouth. "But horseplay can get out of hand. And we—you and I—are responsible for the kids when they're under our supervision. I take that seriously."

"So do I." But somehow Luke had her pegged as irresponsible. Lacking in maturity. Why did that hurt so much? And why did she care what he thought about her, anyway? Like Dwayne and Aunt Jen, he liked things to be the way he wanted them and wasn't much into leaving wiggle room for others.

He scuffed the floor with the toe of his work boot. "I can get this linoleum pulled up for you."

"I can help, too," an unfamiliar voice said quietly from the open doorway leading to the dining room.

Startled, Luke and Delaney turned as one.

Drake Mason.

Delaney shared a quick glance with Luke, then took a smiling step toward the young man. "Drake, how good of you to come."

"But the other kids aren't coming, huh? Because you told them you invited me."

"Some had other commitments today. But—" She didn't want to lie to the boy. Or gloss things over. He wasn't stupid and who knows how much of their conversation he'd overheard?

"To be honest," Luke said, pinning him with a direct look, "that's exactly what's happened, Drake. Your reputation has preceded you. You've been involved in vandalism in the past. And you've picked on my daughter Anna, as well. Thinking you might be here today, she refused to come. The other kids likely rallied around her."

Confusion and alarm flashed through the boy's eyes. "I never picked on Anna."

Luke's jaw hardened and Delaney could tell he was fighting to control his temper. "What would you call shadowing her in the hallways at school?

Trying to grab her backpack away from her? Making kissy sounds in study hall so that the other kids laughed at her? Made fun of her?"

"I…" His face flushing a bright red, Drake stared at Luke's granite-hard expression, then at Delaney. "I… I *like* Anna."

Was he saying he had a *crush* on Luke's daughter?

"I wanted to carry her backpack for her. I—"

"If that's what you're claiming, you need to know right now that your behavior was totally out of line." Luke didn't look to be buying Drake's romantic spin. "That's not how you show someone you like them. Especially a sweet young girl who you repeatedly upset, embarrassed and made hate going to school."

"I didn't mean to do any of that. Honest."

"Well, you did. Actions speak louder than words." He jerked his head in the direction of the front door. "I think it's time you went home, Drake. There's nothing for you to do here today."

The boy turned miserable eyes on Delaney. Hoping he could recruit her into his corner? But this was Luke's issue, not hers, even though her heart went out to the boy, if what he was telling them was true.

After a moment, Drake nodded, then left. The sound of the screen door closing echoed through the house.

"Luke—"

He raised his palm to halt her. "I know what you're going to say. You think I was too hard on him. That I should have found him something to do around here."

"It *is* going to be his home. Isn't it natural that he might be drawn to the place? Want to be a part of fixing it up?"

"If he's here, the other kids won't come back, Delaney. It's as simple as that. Do you want to finish the project by the deadline or is taking up for the underdog—a boy whose history you know nothing about—the route you'd prefer to go?"

"I feel sorry for him."

"Me, too. After all, his father is Benton Mason. But I can't let that cloud my judgment. He's caused a lot of trouble around here and Anna's been targeted in the past."

"Boys sometimes do dumb things when they like a girl."

"Such as?"

She laughed at his puzzled look. "Don't you remember? It can't be *that* long ago since you were a teenager."

He frowned. "You don't seriously think he hounded her like that because he liked her, do you?"

"Maybe. I remember a boy in my math class who I had a crush on when I moved to Canyon Springs. He was a nice boy and I liked him. But he always acted irritated with me, picked arguments. I stayed as far away from him as I could get just to avoid being embarrassed and feeling bad about myself. It wasn't until after graduation that he told me that he *liked* me back then." She shook her head. "The poor kid, he was so socially inept that he couldn't express his true feelings appropriately. Just acted out in behaviors that were totally in opposition to how he really felt."

Luke, standing in that familiar hands-on-his-hip pose, stared down at the ripped-up linoleum.

"Luke? Did you hear what I said?"

"What? Yeah. Sure. I was just thinking, you know, about… Anna."

She nodded, still not feeling good about sending Drake away. "Anna and Travis have previous commitments, but maybe I'll give a few of the others a call to let them know Drake won't be here."

"Kids don't lack for things to do on a holiday weekend, Delaney, and I imagine, like Anna and Travis, they've made plans for the day. And actually…" Luke's eyes reflected an apology in advance. "I think you need to give the project a breather this weekend."

Her eyes widened. Hadn't all along Luke expressed doubts that the work could be completed in the allotted time frame? How could he suggest further delay?

"We can't afford to lose another day of work." She motioned to her clipboard checklist on the countertop. "While I'm popping over to visit my aunt Jen as often as I can on weekdays, there aren't many Saturdays left after today and one of those I'm in a wedding in Canyon Springs."

"I realize that, but I also recognize that I'm partially responsible for at least some of the kids being no-shows today, including my own. You need to give me the opportunity to make some phone calls. Talk to a few parents. Some of the kids."

"But—"

"And," he interrupted, his solemn gaze now warming, "I need your permission to deliver some motivation to get the kids back on board."

Bribery again.

But what exactly did Luke Hunter have in mind?

Chapter Twelve

"I like the sound of that, Vinnie. I never thought I'd be calling myself a Kansan and certainly not by the end of the summer, but God works in mysterious ways. I'll be talking to you later. Thanks for calling. I look forward to working with you guys."

Luke shut off the phone and relaxed into a kitchen chair. It was settled. He'd made a decision. Had a direction. It felt good. *Thank You, Lord.*

He'd spent way too many years after Marsha's death drifting. Not from place to place, but emotionally. Mentally. Spiritually. Going with the flow and not taking responsibility for his life. How had he become so passive? That had never been his nature, even as a boy.

But Marsha…that had changed him in ways he wasn't proud of. Is that why his dad and Grady never challenged him to take on more at the Hideaway? Nor were they open to his recent rumblings of wanting additional responsibility. Didn't they think he could handle it?

But Josh and Vinnie knew what he was capable of. Knew he could carry his share of the load. They'd pulled each other out of the line of fire more than once. Depended on each other. Trusted each other.

He glanced down at his watch and smiled. 5:30 a.m. Vinnie always forgot that their time difference in the summer was two hours rather than one. Good thing he was an early riser, even on a Saturday morning. It had taken all week for him, working alongside Delaney at the project house, to convince her a youth group trail ride this morning would be a good move to get the kids back on board. Bribery, she still called it. But she could laugh about it now, which made him smile, too.

For a long moment he listened to the silence, unbroken except by the cheerful chirp of a sparrow outside the open kitchen window above the sink. He loved this time of day when the thick stand of pines shadowed the cabin, fresh mountain air cooled the forest, and before the wind picked up. He'd missed the high country when he'd been in the military, especially when in the desert regions of remote locales. He'd miss it again, no doubt, when relocated.

But it was good to have the decision made.

He rose resolutely and looked around the kitchen where he and his children had shared meals together the past six years. He didn't regret bringing them back here from where he'd been stationed in Texas. It had been the right thing to do. But it was time to move on, to see what God had in store.

Unbidden, the smiling face of Delaney Marks surfaced in his thoughts and his chest tightened. No, Delaney wasn't in God's plans for him. Appealing as she might be, as warm and loving as she'd been to his kids, neither she—nor any other woman—would be joining him in this new venture.

He flipped off the kitchen light and headed slowly into the still-shadowed living room area of the cabin, lost in his thoughts.

Until he heard a sniffle.

He reached out for the wall switch to illuminate the room. And there they all sat. His children. Sitting on the sofa like ravens rowed up on a power line. Glaring at him.

He frowned. "What's wrong?"

"Anna heard you, Dad." Travis's voice held a dangerous edge. "About Kansas. When were you going to tell us?"

So much for finding the right time for a heart-to-heart. "Nothing had been finalized. There wasn't anything to tell."

"It sounds as if there's something to tell now." Travis crossed his arms, his eyes accusing.

Anna nodded solemnly. Chloe sniffed again. She'd been crying.

Drawing in a breath, he let it out slowly, then moved to scoop his youngest daughter into his arms and sat down on the sofa by Anna. She scooted away from him.

He closed his eyes for a moment, willing away the flashback to another time when he'd gathered his children around him, Chloe snuggled in his arms just like now. A child on either side of him. Travis barely eleven, Anna nine, Chloe two. He'd met them at the home of friends where Marsha had sent them off for a sleepover the evening of her fateful decision. Holding them close, he did by far the hardest thing he'd ever done in his life— broke the tragic news of their mother's untimely death to them. A reality that he could barely comprehend himself at the time.

Shoving away the too-vivid memory, he opened his eyes. Thankfully, this was nothing like that time. Nothing. This was good news that, once they got used to the idea, would open happy doors to the future for all of them.

"Let me start by saying that there are things in life that you may not always understand until you're older.

Travis sighed as he leaned his elbow on the farside sofa arm, resting his jaw in his open palm. "Don't give us that old song and dance. We can understand more than you give us credit for. Even Chloe."

Luke's littlest sniffled again and he kissed the top of her head. Wiped away a stray tear. He should reprimand Travis for his tone. His disrespect. But that could wait. Clearly Luke's eldest had been caught off-guard. That was his fault.

Luke made a point of looking each of his kids in the eye. Travis, nearly a man. Anna, his rough-and-tumble tomboy. And sweet Chloe, who most resembled her mother. His heart swelled. *I love these kids, Lord. They are a part of me and Marsha, the product of the love we once shared. Please let them understand that I would never in my life ever do anything that I thought would harm them.*

He shifted Chloe in his lap. "You remember me talking about my army buddies, Josh and Vinnie, right?"

All nodded. They'd heard plenty about those two larger-than-life guys through the years. The funny stuff, of course. No war front stories.

"They're from Kansas, and several years ago they started a business that's growing steadily. Up until now they've had the financial and accounting work outsourced, but now they could use another partner to oversee that in-house."

Josh and Vinnie, thankfully, understood he didn't have cash to invest and couldn't take out loans with Travis and Anna nearing college age. But they were good with that.

"They want you." Anna's lower lip trembled.

He met her gaze evenly, encouragingly. "That's right. You may not remember, but before we came to Hunter Ridge, I held a lot of important jobs in the military. Had a lot of responsibility."

"And you were gone all the time, too," Travis mumbled. "I remember that."

A muscle tightened in Luke's throat at the accusation. But it wasn't one he could refute. He had been gone a lot, and maybe if he hadn't...

"You probably made good money, too," Anna echoed, ever conscious of their limited finances, clipping coupons, shopping on a budget.

Luke frowned as he brushed back the sleep-disheveled hair from Chloe's face. "Decent enough. But it's more than that."

"Like what, Dad?" Travis shot to his feet. "We don't want to go to Kansas."

Chloe's lower lip protruded. "Anna says they don't have mountains there. How do people live without mountains, Daddy?"

He gave her a reassuring squeeze, hoping to stave off more tears. "People all over the country live without mountains, sweetheart."

"I don't want to."

Travis gave him a look. "Maybe you can just walk off and turn your back on Delaney, but I'm not leaving Scottie behind. So you can forget that."

An invisible fist punched Luke in the stomach. *Delaney?* What did she have to do with this?

Shock must have registered on his face, because Travis snorted. "We know you like her, Dad. She likes you, too. What's the big secret?"

"Dad." Anna lightly touched his arm and he turned to look into her sorrowful eyes. "I don't want to leave Grandma and Grandpa. Or Grandma Jo. Or Thunder."

Her horse.

He reached out to take her hand, offering a consoling smile, but his mind raced, stalled, raced again at his son's matter-of-fact conclusion regarding Delaney. "It's not as if we're moving to the moon, honey. We'll be back for holidays. Summer vacation. I promise."

She looked away, blinking rapidly, and he drew a heavy breath. This was not going as planned. He'd intended to do research on the area, on the fun things to do there so they'd be excited about it. But if the kids were reacting like this, he'd better be prepared for Mom and Grandma. Ready to do damage control.

"We don't even get a vote on this?" Anna still wasn't looking at him, but Travis's glare did double duty.

"You know I love you, don't you?" He drew Chloe close, squeezed Anna's hand. "Sometimes dads have to make unpopular decisions for the best of a family. Remember how at first none of you wanted to come to Hunter Ridge? But it will work out. Good things will come of it and someday you'll look back and see why this was a good thing for all of us."

Travis rolled his eyes. "Yeah, right."

"There are good universities in that area of the Midwest, Trav. Nebraska. Kansas State. University of Kansas. Mizzou." He'd make sure Travis got the opportunities his father hadn't been given.

"That's nice and I hope you have a great life there, Dad. But I'm not going to Kansas. So bon voyage."

Travis spun on his barefooted heel and headed down the hallway to his room.

When Luke heard a light knock at the door, he groaned. The youth group was here already?

"Delaney!" With a gasp, Anna leaped up and stared down in horror at her pajamas. "And my hair!"

Chloe squirmed in his arms, escaping from his lap to race to the door.

And all he could do was prop his elbows on his knees and lower his face into his hands.

We know you like her. She likes you, too. So what's the big secret?

"Delaney! You're here! You're here!" The little girl hopped from foot to foot, almost dancing with excitement. "And you look beautiful!"

"Thank you." As she stepped inside, Delaney couldn't help but notice Chloe's reddened eyes and sniffling nose. Must be one of those days in the Hunter household. How on earth did Luke manage?

She pulled out a tissue from her pocket and

handed it to Chloe, barely glimpsing a pajama-clad Anna disappearing down a hallway. No sign of Travis. But a weary-looking Luke was rising from the sofa.

"Good morning, Luke."

"If you say so."

Oh, dear.

"Is the youth group here already?" He glanced out the picture window. "I thought they weren't coming until seven."

"I'm an hour early. Anna called me last night and said she wanted to show me around before we went riding." She placed a gentle hand on Chloe's shoulder. "If this isn't a good time, I can come back later."

His brow wrinkled. "No, no, timing is fine. That is if you don't mind waiting for Chloe and Anna to get dressed. We had...there were...un-expected delays this morning."

"If you're sure."

"It's fine. Could I get you coffee or something? We're hosting breakfast when we get back from our ride, but I could fix toast or cereal if you're hungry."

"I don't want to ruin my appetite. I've heard Hunter's Hideaway puts on quite a spread."

"That we do."

Chloe reached for Delaney's hand with both of hers. "Isn't Delaney beautiful, Daddy?"

A smile reluctantly surfaced at Chloe's broken-record assessment, but he didn't look at Delaney. "Yes, honey, like a princess. Now run on back to your room and get dressed and we'll see what we can do about that hair of yours."

Chloe reached up to hug Delaney, then took off.

He gave her a halfhearted smile. "Sorry we're not ready."

"No problem." She drew her gaze away from his to look around the cabin. Golden-toned log walls, raftered ceiling, a big iron woodstove. No feminine touches, though—had this not been the home he'd shared with his wife? Garrett hadn't divulged details and she hadn't wanted to pry, but likely not.

Nevertheless, the room held appeal with a patterned rug on the wooden floor and a poster-size photograph of the San Francisco Peaks near Flagstaff gracing one of the walls. "I like this. It feels so rustic."

He roughed up the hair on the back of his head. "That's putting it nicely."

"I'm serious. I love the simplicity. Log cabins have such charm."

"Hunter's Hideaway has its fair share of them nestled back here in the pines. They've been a long-time staple of the property, first for sportsmen, then later also for guests wanting to explore off-the-beaten path mountain country on horseback or foot."

"I hate to admit it, but although I lived in Canyon Springs for quite a few years and heard of Hunter Ridge, I'd never been here before. And yet Hunter's Hideaway looks like quite a complex—a general store, an inn, horseback riding. It's kind of hidden away in the forest, a few steps outside the heart of town."

"That's what gave it its name." He moved to a window and pulled open the drapes to admit the morning sun. "We try to stay low-key and don't do a whole lot of promotion. Hunter Ridge has always been about word-of-mouth, not media hype. We aren't big on turning the place into Disneyland. There are way too many folks who don't take the backcountry seriously. They come up here and get themselves in a whole lot of trouble."

"I've seen that in the news many times. Search-and-rescue teams are kept hopping, sometimes without a happy ending."

He motioned for her to follow him into the kitchen where he poured himself a mug of coffee. "Sure you don't want some?"

"No, thank you." She studied the log-walled room, the polished wooden trestle table, tiled floor, the cast-iron and copper cooking utensils hanging above the butcher-block island. She'd love to cook in a cute kitchen like this. "Getting back to your comment about not wanting Hunter Ridge to be Disneyland. Is that one of the reasons people around here don't care for the influx of artists?

I've heard that they hope to increase promotion, bring more visitors in to expand their market."

"Sunshine tell you that?" He took another sip of coffee.

"What? That people around here don't care for artists or that local artists hope to lure in more outsiders? Actually, she mentioned both."

"Figures. They probably want to turn this into another Sedona with wall-to-wall shoppers, but at least winter at a few thousand feet higher than that community should prevent that from happening to any great degree. At least for half of the year anyway."

She moved around the room, studying framed photos on the wall, acutely conscious of Luke's gaze following her. There was Travis as a youngster holding up a fish he'd caught. Anna on a pony, looking determined to stay on. Chloe cuddling a kitten.

Was that a photo of Luke and his wife with their kids on the far wall? But she didn't cross the room to check it out.

She turned back to Luke. "I'm sorry to have barged in on you so early this morning. I should have asked to speak to you when Anna called last night. You know, to make sure her invitation was okay with you. I feel as though I walked into the middle of something."

He offered a self-conscious smile. "Don't worry about it. Kids are kids."

And no doubt dads were dads. Something had disturbed him in a major way if she wasn't misreading the somewhat bleak look in his eyes.

As the silence stretched, she searched for a topic of conversation. "It's a beautiful morning."

"It is."

"Thanks for arranging this outing for the kids. And for making those phone calls." He'd had a long talk with Anna and Travis, too, about the possibility of Drake joining them to work on the house, explaining how he or Delaney would be there if Drake's behavior became inappropriate. They didn't like it, but agreed that the boy should be given another chance. Now if she could only get Luke on that same wavelength regarding Benton.

He set his mug on the island. "You're still good with it? Didn't just give in?"

They'd discussed it at great length last weekend, Luke having decided that since no kids showed up, he'd hang around all morning to get the layers of linoleum flooring ripped out in the kitchen. He'd returned a few times throughout the week to continue on the bathrooms and entry while she painted the kitchen cabinets.

Occasionally he brought Chloe who played quietly on the porch with her plastic horses, and

Anna and Travis popped in once to drop off pizza for their lunch. Working in different areas of the house while the exterior painters labored on, they weren't tripping over each other, but saw each other enough to keep up a running conversation. Nothing too personal, but comfortable enough that it left Delaney smiling to herself when she shut off the lights each night.

"Like I said earlier, I'd prefer that kids—and adults—not always be motivated by 'what's in it for me.' But maybe this will be a fresh start for all of us—heading over to the project after breakfast with an added emphasis on being a cheerful giver."

His eyes warmed. "From what I've seen, you're always a cheerful giver, aren't you, Delaney?"

Was he making fun of her? "I try to be. God says it's more blessed to give than to receive."

"He does at that."

Luke glanced toward the kitchen door just as Anna and Chloe appeared, both in jeans, T-shirts, Western boots and windbreakers, their hair pulled back into ponytails.

"I'm sorry we weren't ready when you got here." Anna didn't acknowledge or so much as look at her father, signaling again to Delaney that her arrival had interrupted something.

Chloe stretched out one hand to snare Delaney's—and one to her dad. "You're coming, too, aren't you, Daddy?"

"I think he has other things to do," Anna said quickly, heading back into the living room.

The sadness in Luke's eyes tore at Delaney's heart.

"Come with us, Luke," she encouraged. "The girls want to show me around and you'll know the history behind everything."

His grateful gaze met hers, but even with Chloe tugging at his hand, he looked undecided.

"The youth group is due to start arriving in forty-five minutes," she coaxed, "so it won't take long."

"I don't think Anna wants me tagging along."

"She'll get over it." Smiling down at Chloe, she gave the small hand a squeeze, then looked up with an impish gaze at the girl's handsome daddy. "Come on, Luke, don't be an old fuddy-duddy."

Chapter Thirteen

Fuddy-duddy. Holding the door open to the Inn at Hunter's Hideaway for Delaney, Anna and Chloe to enter, Luke could laugh at that now. Sort of. Mostly because the look in Delaney's sparkling eyes belied her taunting words.

The kids said she liked him. He'd known that from day one when she'd dazzled him with that flirty smile of hers. And he had to admit he'd enjoyed working alongside her at the project house this past week. He felt so guilty about running the kids off a few Saturdays ago, that helping out was the least he could do to make up for it. But what he found disturbing was that his children concluded he liked her as well. Travis had even hinted that moving to Kansas would be tantamount to turning his back on her.

That was crazy. How had it gotten by him that the kids were reading more into his helping with the youth project than he'd been aware? He'd worked on it other years, hadn't he?

"Grandma! Grandma!" Grasping Delaney's hand to drag her forward, Chloe charged toward his mother, Elaine Hunter, who looked up from something she was working on at the reception desk. "This is Delaney, Grandma!"

His mother glanced at him curiously, then came around the desk for introductions. Mom looked great this morning in jeans, a blue plaid shirt, and a tan leather vest, her sandy brown, side-parted hair grazing her shoulders. Trim and vibrant, nobody would ever guess that she'd just turned sixty.

"I'm Elaine. Known as Mom to this one—" She nodded to Luke, then motioned to his daughters. "And Grandma to these two. Anna told me last night that she planned to give you the grand tour this morning."

Mom had no doubt heard more about Delaney than she cared to. The girls had been talking about her at Sunday dinner with his folks for weeks. How pretty she was. How nice. How cool her hair and clothes were. He'd kept out of it, doing his best to avoid Rio's smirking smile and dodge Grady's booted foot kicking him under the table.

"This place is amazing." Delaney's eyes sparkled with characteristic enthusiasm. "Your husband pointed out the buildings and trails on that humongous wall map. Over two hundred wooded acres bumped up against endless national forest property? Grady let me peek in one of the unoccupied cabins, too. And Rio and J.C. showed me around the stable and corrals. Thirty horses? Wow."

"She thinks the surrey is *romantic*." Anna, now

standing behind Delaney, gave him a sidelong, accusatory look. He'd better have a talk with the kids about the status of his relationship with the pretty blonde sooner rather than later.

"So *this* is Delaney," a familiar voice said warmly from the top of the stairs. All eyes turned to see Grandma Jo gracefully descending. Leave it to her to make a grand entrance. When she reached the bottom, she came forward to shake Delaney's outstretched hand. "My great-granddaughters have told me a lot about you. Welcome to the Hideaway."

"Grandma Jo—Josephine—is my dad's mother," Luke provided. Even with his two other "middle" sisters absent, it must be confusing for Delaney having an army of Hunters coming out of the woodwork to greet her as if she were some kind of celebrity. Which made him wonder that else the kids had been saying about Delaney. And him.

"It's good to meet you, too." Delaney then nodded in the direction of his mother. "I was just telling Elaine how impressed I am with this entire operation. I'll definitely be back to check out the general store treasures when I have time to linger."

"You'll like the homemade chocolate chip cookies best," Chloe chimed in, then quietly sidled over to lean against him. Smiling down at her, he slipped his arm around her shoulders. His baby.

"There's much to see here," Grandma Jo agreed, "much more than a whirlwind tour can do justice, so feel welcome to come back as often as you'd like. We're always happy to see new faces, especially one as pretty as yours."

Color rose in Delaney's cheeks as she murmured a thank-you. Grandma had always been a hospitable sort, but wasn't she laying it on a bit thick?

"It's my understanding," Grandma continued, "that you're here for the summer to work with the church youth group and supervise their project. How is that coming along?"

Delaney glanced briefly at Luke. "We're mostly finished with the outdoor work, so when the monsoons come in, we'll be okay there. Today, after breakfast, we'll begin stripping wallpaper and doing general cleanup in preparation for the next phase."

"A worthwhile endeavor. No family should have to live apart as they've had to this past year."

Looking up at him, Chloe's eyes suddenly pooled with tears as the impact of her great-grandma's words jolted her memory.

"Grandma Jo—" Her lower lip quivered as she appealed to the family matriarch, and a knot tightened in Luke's stomach when curious eyes turned to his youngest. "This morning Daddy told us—"

With a laugh, he gently slipped his hand over her mouth. "Let's save that for later, okay, sweetheart?"

Surprised, she looked up at him, tears stopped

in their tracks. He lifted her into his arms where she looped her legs around his waist, then he turned to the still-open door behind them. "Looks like the kids are arriving. What do you say we go see if Rio has your pony saddled up?"

Eyes brightening, she nodded, the move to Kansas forgotten. He gave her a hug, grateful that she'd allowed him to divert her attention. Although acutely aware of the questioning stares—and Anna's glare—now was not the time or place to announce his plans to the rest of his family.

Anna brushed by him and headed out the door to greet her friends.

He caught Delaney's eye. "Ready to go?"

Curiosity lit her eyes, too, but she nodded, said goodbye to his mother and grandmother, then followed him outside. He pulled the door shut and they moved away from the inn.

Close call. But no doubt he'd be grilled at the first opportunity.

Nevertheless, with a relieved grin, he gave Chloe another grateful hug and set her on the ground. Legs pumping and ponytail flying, she dashed off in search of Rio. Man, how he loved that kid. He glanced at Delaney only to discover she was openly studying him. His smile faltered.

"What?"

"Nothing."

Yeah, right. "You ready to ride, then?"

For a moment, he thought she was going to

ask him point-blank what Chloe had been about to blurt out. But instead, she flashed a smile that always made him weak in the knees.

"I haven't been on a horse since I was a teenager, but there's no way I'd let the youth group go on this adventure without me."

"So let's go." He stretched out his hand to her. Then, as her gaze flickered in question to his, he self-consciously let it drop to his side. She wasn't one of his kids that he needed to hang on to, keep close, safe. But although he'd once taken her hand to help her up from the kitchen floor, what would it feel like snuggled in his with their fingers entwined?

Don't go there.

All the talk earlier that morning of her liking him and him liking her and *what's the big secret* had befuddled his brain. But it didn't change a thing. Not one thing.

"How's it going?" Travis reined his chestnut mare back to where Delaney brought up the caboose end of the fifteen trail riders. For the past three-quarters of an hour, the horses and riders had eased into a comfortable distance from each other along a well-worn path under overarching pines. Leather creaking. Bits jangling. Sunlight dappled down on the coolish morning, making her thankful for her light jacket.

She reined her dapple gray, Chiffon, to the side

to make more room for Travis and his mount. "I haven't ridden for a long time."

"No foolin'? I'd never have guessed."

She lowered her brows in mock reprimand. "Lying is a sin as much as stealing."

Travis grinned. Then sobering, he lowered his voice. "I, uh, owe you an apology, Delaney."

She tilted her head in question as he shifted in the saddle. Adjusted his reins.

"You know," he continued, "for the way I acted that first night we met at your place. For a few other times, too. I'm sorry. You didn't deserve to be the brunt of my bad attitude."

Had Luke talked to him? Or had he initiated this on his own?

"I imagine you were disappointed that the college intern couldn't come for the summer."

"Not so much. It's more that—" He leaned forward to pat his horse on the neck, then straightened in the saddle to look off into the forest. Shrugged. "Never mind."

"It's that your dad was there, isn't it?"

His gaze met hers in surprise—and confirmation.

"Always. Ever since Mom—" He cut himself short and again looked away, ramrod-straight and eyes fixed on his father farther up the trail.

They rode in silence for several minutes, a raven crying out above them, hooves sounding hollowly on the dirt path, bits of conversation drifting back from the others. But she could almost tangibly feel the heartache emanating from the young man riding next to her.

"I'm sorry," she said, her words coming quietly, "about the loss of your mother, Travis."

She always hesitated, when someone shared such a loss, to chime in about her own, not wanting to diminish the other person's grief or draw attention to herself.

He turned an uncertain gaze on her. "You know that she—"

At her nod, relief flickered through his eyes. He'd have been about eleven years old when his mother had taken her life. What did that do to a boy just on the brink of adolescence? A first child who would have had more time to bond with his mother than had his younger siblings. Garrett said Luke didn't like talking about the loss and didn't like others talking about it. Did that extend to his kids, as well?

"Don't get me wrong." Travis shifted in the saddle again. "It was cool when I was a kid to have Dad so involved in everything I did. You know, school events. Church camp. Boy Scouts. But it's getting…old."

This was a young man clearly ready to cut a few apron strings.

Travis clucked to his horse. "Sometimes I feel that after losing Mom, he thinks he has to be there every second to make sure nothing bad happens to me ever again. I've had money saved for over a year to buy a used truck, but he won't give me the go-ahead."

"You've talked to him about this?"

Travis cast her a doubtful look. "And hurt his feelings?"

He loved his dad. Felt protective of him. "I think the way you react to his involvement, like that night at youth group, hurts him more than being honest would."

"We don't communicate that well anymore. And with him wanting us to leave Hunter Ridge? Well, we had a few words this morning and it wasn't pretty. But no way am I going to Kansas."

Kansas?

Delaney's hands tightened on the reins. Had that been what she'd unintentionally barged in on a few hours ago? That news would no doubt have been enough to alienate Anna and could account for what Chloe had been about to blurt to her great-grandmother before Luke expertly cut her off. "Your father wants to move away from here? Why?"

"Who knows? He has a job offer from some of his old army buddies. Says it's for the best and that someday, when we're older, we'll understand."

Best for whom? Him or his kids?

How could he even consider taking them away from Hunter Ridge? Far from the Hideaway where they were surrounded by a loving family. She'd been introduced to a number of them this morning. All had greeted her as though welcoming a long-lost friend. She'd give just about anything to have a family like that nearby. Couldn't he see that he had something special here that others could only dream of?

"I'm sorry, Travis. I know your dad planning a move must have come as a shock."

"No kidding."

Now that they could again glimpse the main buildings of the property through the trees, up ahead Travis's father had reined to a halt, allowing the string of riders to file past him as he waited for her and Travis to catch up.

When they reached him, Travis rode past him without a word, and Luke reined in beside her. Looking yummy in a Western-cut shirt, jeans and boots, his eyes were shadowed by the brim of a cowboy hat. What was it about a Western hat that made an already handsome man even more masculine and rugged?

Luke nodded toward the teens now well ahead of them. "I hope that conversation between the two of you included an apology from Travis."

"It did. A sincere one." But she wouldn't share anything else Travis had said, though she wanted to question Luke on his decision to leave Hunter Ridge.

"Like I said earlier, he's a good kid. But sometimes…" Luke shook his head, a bemused smile surfacing.

"Parenting isn't for wimps?"

"Single-parenting sure isn't."

That was the first direct reference to his solo status that he'd made since she'd met him. Her gaze held his steadily, hoping he'd elaborate.

"My wife—the kids' mother—died a few years back. Six, actually."

"I'm sorry. That must make parenting doubly difficult." Could memories of his deceased wife be too much to live with here? Familiar faces and places shared might comfort some people, but only serve to torment others. Her own family had moved frequently, so there was no hometown filled with memories of Mom, Dad, Grandma and Tiffany. Canyon Springs with her aunt was as close to a hometown as she'd ever gotten.

"I thought you should know." He stared down the trail, a muscle tightening in his jaw. "You know, since my kids are working on the Mason house with you."

"I'll do my best not to say or do something that might be insensitive to their situation." Thankfully, Garrett had already clued her in so she hadn't assumed they had a mother in their lives.

"I do appreciate your help on the project," she ventured, "but please don't feel obligated to make it your responsibility. I'm sure you already have enough to do, and I know you have reservations about the Masons."

"We've made the youth group project a family event since Travis entered high school. I'm good with it."

"I know from my own experiences..." She wanted to word this carefully. "That working on a project like this can be a real growing experience for young people. It provides opportunities for casual conversation about personal and spiritual issues that might not take place otherwise. But for some kids, the presence of parents can make them self-conscious, uncomfortable sharing their innermost thoughts, feelings and fears."

The Sunday night Bible study discussions hadn't gone beyond canned answers and superficialities with Luke again plopped in their midst. She didn't expect it to be any different tomorrow night. But Travis certainly wouldn't have shared with her what he did today had his father been riding next to them.

Luke adjusted the reins, a troubled look in his eyes. "You don't think parents should spend time with their kids?"

"Of course I do. And I appreciate having another adult on the premises at Bible studies, outings and projects. I think that's a good practice in this day and age." She leaned over to pat her horse's neck. "Maybe parents could take turns, not be present for all work sessions, or every event."

He shifted in the saddle, his eyes narrowing in her direction. "Exactly what did Travis say to you?"

"What do you mean?"

"Did he tell you he doesn't want me there?"

She cringed inwardly. She should have waited until later to talk to Luke about this so he wouldn't have tied the conversation directly back to his son. Dumb, dumb, dumb.

"I'm thinking of all the kids in the youth group who need a taste of independence while under their parents' roof. An opportunity to grow and learn and escape the nest once in a while, to stretch their wings while still having the safety net of family."

Luke was silent a moment, then angled a considering look at her. "And you know this how? From your years of parenting experience?"

She reined her horse to a halt. Luke did likewise. "I may not be a parent, Luke, but I am deeply aware of what it takes to be a good one. An excellent one, in fact. I learned firsthand from the best—my own parents and my grandparents. From church couples whom I've long admired, as well, and try to emulate in my relationships with children."

His brows rose at her mild reprimand.

If he expected her to agree that merely producing a biological child suddenly made someone—him—an expert at parenting, trumping the life experience of growing up in a super-*functional* family, he'd better not hold his breath.

"Don't tell me you haven't thought it," she prodded gently when he didn't respond. "Haven't thought that I'm too young, too inexperienced, too childless to know what I'm doing."

Guilt flickered through his eyes.

Just what she thought.

"Luke, I'm not telling you how to raise your family. I wouldn't presume to do that. Your children are wonderful and you're doing a great job with them. But it may be time to loosen your grip just a bit."

For a moment his eyes lit with anger, then, just as quickly, that pervasive, underlying sadness surfaced again. Her heart wrenched, knowing she was responsible for it. In defense of herself, she'd gone too far. With the upset he'd had with his kids earlier that morning, he didn't need to hear this, too.

But, oh, how desperately she wanted to give him a hug. To take him in her arms and reassure him that all would be well. That he didn't have to try so hard with his kids to make sure that no harm came to them.

That was God's job.

"Think about it. Please?"

Appearing deep in thought, she wasn't sure

he'd heard her whispered words. But not knowing what else to say, what else to do, she gently nudged her horse's sides and moved on down the tree-lined trail.

Chapter Fourteen

"**I** love horses," Chloe stated matter-of-factly, drawing Luke's attention to his daughter seated beside him at the big, pine-shaded picnic table behind the inn. "I'm going to be a cowboy when I grow up."

Travis, on the other side of her, slipped his arm around her shoulders. "You can't be a cow*boy,* Chloe. You're a girl."

The teens gathered at their table laughed, but not in a ridiculing way. They liked Chloe and treated her like a much-loved younger sibling.

Chloe raised her chin with the dignity of a princess. "Aunt Rio says some of the best cowboys *are* girls. So there."

Seated across from Delaney at the only place available by the time he got there, Luke forked up a slice of sausage. "That sounds like your aunt Rio."

Chloe studied Delaney curiously. "When you were eight years old, what did you want to be when you grew up?"

All eyes turned to her with interest, including Luke's.

"Let's see, eight years old." She narrowed her eyes in thought. "I think, after my folks took me to a rodeo in Prescott at about that age I wanted to be…"

She paused for dramatic effect.

"A barrel racer!" Chloe cried triumphantly, delighted to have someone else on her, Anna's and Rio's side.

"No, not a barrel racer," Delaney teased as she paused again, obviously enjoying keeping them in suspense. "A…rodeo clown."

All the kids except Chloe laughed. Luke sent Delaney an amused look, grateful to make a less serious connection with her after their too-recent conversation about parenting. "Why am I not surprised?"

"Girls can be rodeo clowns," Chloe defended. "They are brave and can run fast and make people laugh, too."

"What do you want to be when *you* grow up, Luke?" Delaney countered, an impish gleam now lighting her eyes. Had she hated as much as he did that awkward stretch of time after they'd returned from the ride and got the horses put away and the kids settled in to eat? "I mean, what *did* you want to be when you were a kid?"

Travis snickered. "Grandma Jo says he wanted to be a superhero."

Luke drew back in mock offense. "What's so funny about that? You don't think I'd look good in a cape and tights?"

Groaning, Travis placed his elbows on the table and lowered his face into his hands. "Thanks a lot, Dad. That's a visual we all could have done without."

Laughing, Nelson stood and grabbed his brother by the back of his sweatshirt collar. "Hey, I have to get back to town and run a few errands before I can meet everybody over at the Mason house. And since you drove…"

With a promise to meet at the project location by ten o'clock, the teens stacked their plates, cups and utensils at the end of the table before departing. Chloe leaped up and charged past her uncle Grady as he stepped outside a back door with two heavy-duty, oversize plastic tubs.

Eyeing the dishes, Grady gave a low whistle as he approached. "Looks like a swarm of locusts of Biblical proportion hit this place."

He winked at Delaney, ever the lady's man.

Luke shook his head. *Back off, little brother.* "Thanks for scheduling us in on such short notice."

"No problem." With Luke's help, Grady loaded the bins. Then he picked up one of the overflowing tubs and nodded to the other. "Can you get that one when you're done here?"

"Sure."

Grady started to walk away, then set the tub down again and pulled a folded envelope from a back jeans pocket. He dropped it in front of Anna. "This was in the mail when I picked it up last night. Sorry I didn't get it sorted out until this morning."

As he headed back inside, Luke's daughter stared down at the envelope. Then with a gasp, she snatched it up and ripped it open.

"Whatcha have there?" Luke craned his neck. "A love letter?"

"Get real, Dad." Anna's anxious eyes scanned the pages with barely concealed excitement.

Luke met Delaney's questioning gaze, then he shrugged as he lifted the coffee cup to his lips and settled in to wait for his daughter to enlighten them.

"I can't believe this," Anna finally said, her words coming softly and Luke again exchanged a glance with Delaney. Then Anna abruptly stood and tossed the papers to the table in front of her. "I give up. Why even try?"

Luke set his cup on the table. "What's the problem?"

"My English teacher insisted I enter this stupid poetry contest. But I didn't even make the finals." She motioned to the papers. "Someone at the contest wrote all over it in red pen, marking stuff out, writing stuff in."

Anna wrote poetry?

Delaney stretched out her hand. "Can I look at it?"

Anna hesitated, then stepped back from the table. "Go ahead, if you feel like gagging."

Delaney reached for the papers and spread them out before her, reading silently as Anna hovered nearby. When she finally looked up and smiled into his daughter's anxious eyes, Luke gave an inward sigh of relief.

"This poem is good, Anna. The metaphor is compelling and tugs at the heart. Your words are fresh and evocative, and the rhythm and alliteration are well suited to free verse."

Anna's hopeful gaze searched hers, drinking in the praise but clearly afraid to accept it.

Luke folded his forearms on the table and leaned forward. "It sounds as if you know something about poetry, Delaney."

"I used to write a lot of it. I loved my English classes." She looked again to Anna. "I can see why your teacher wanted you to enter it."

At the mention of the contest, the hope in Anna's eyes extinguished. "The judge thinks it stinks."

"I disagree." Delaney pointed to the margin. "Look at that smiley face. And over here, 'well done' and at the bottom, 'this shows promise.' I don't think the intention is to trash it, but you have to remember that this is only one person's opinion. It's up to you to decide what you agree with. What you disagree with. Then make only the changes you want to make."

His daughter made a face. "I'm not making any changes. I didn't expect to win. I'm done with it."

Despite the denial, however, she clearly *had* expected—or at least hoped—to win.

"Some of the most famous poets and writers who ever lived," Delaney said gently, "were rejected over and over before they were finally published and won readers' hearts."

"I hate writing poetry. I only did it for a stupid class." Anna held out her hand for the pages and Delaney reluctantly returned them to her. Anna stuffed them back in the envelope.

"Thanks for saying nice things, Delaney. But you didn't have to." Then without a backward glance, she marched off. Would she tear the poem to shreds or tearfully and tenderly tuck it away somewhere in her room?

Luke toyed with his coffee cup, heart aching, as he watched Anna disappear in the direction of their cabin. Should he go after her or give her some time? He never seemed to know the right thing to do these days. How much simpler it had been when his children were toddlers. You kissed a boo-boo and you were good to go.

"What's the poem about?" Anna hadn't shared it with him, but hopefully Delaney saw no harm in enlightening her father.

She didn't hesitate. "A lost little girl trying to find her way home."

His eyes searched hers. "Anna?"

She nodded. "I think so."

"I worry about her. She keeps so much bottled up inside. Several times today I've seen more emotion come out of her than in a good long while."

"Her poem could use polishing, but it's very good. Your daughter is a deep thinker and in touch with her feelings. Some of the comments in the margin, the ones I didn't draw attention to, were callous in my opinion. I don't want this rather insensitive critique to discourage her from expressing herself that way in the future."

Luke gripped his coffee cup in both hands, studying Delaney. "Any lessons learned?"

"Unfortunately, I don't think she's ready to recognize, let alone embrace, any lessons yet."

"Actually, I was referring to *your* situation, not Anna's."

From the look in her eyes, his words had caught her off-guard. "What do you mean?"

"I noticed you still aren't wearing any of your jewelry." He motioned to her hands splayed flat on the table. "So I assume you're making no attempt to climb back in the saddle after Sunshine Carston turned you down. Am I wrong?"

She lifted her chin slightly. "That's different."

"How so?"

"I happen to be an adult facing the facts. But

I don't want something Anna put a lot of herself into being squashed by a rather harsh critique." She clasped her hands in front of her on the top of the table. "Anna's poem is touching and came from the heart. She's a young girl with talent and dreams that deserve an opportunity to blossom."

"So big girls," he said softly, his gaze holding hers, "can't have talents and dreams that deserve to blossom, too?"

Delaney couldn't help but stare into Luke's eyes.

He took a determined breath. "Don't let Sunshine Carston dampen your enthusiasm. What is it you told Anna? That's only one person's opinion. Everybody needs to have a dream, don't they?"

"Do you?" she countered, not wanting to talk about what her jewelry making meant to her. How it had filled the lonely hours after the death of her family. How it hurt to have it turned down by the Artists' Co-op.

He looked slightly taken aback. "Sure. To see my kids happy and healthy and growing up close to God."

With a soft laugh, she tucked her hands in her lap. "That makes my rodeo clown aspirations sound rather superficial, doesn't it?"

A smile tugged at the corner of his mouth. "There would be a lot fewer happy, healthy and whole bull riders roaming the country if it weren't for those clowns."

"True, but—"

"Hey, you two!" Luke's mother called from the back door. "We're loading the dishwashers, so if you would be so kind, please bring in that last tub so everyone will have something to eat off of at lunchtime."

Luke lifted his hand in acknowledgment and stood as his mother disappeared inside once again. He hefted the tub, then gazed down at Delaney. "The dream thing, Delaney? Think about it."

So turnabout was fair play? She could hardly refuse, having left him with a similar mandate not but an hour ago.

"Echo Ridge Outpost," she blurted, unable to keep the secret any longer, "has taken some of my jewelry on consignment."

"You don't say." He looked genuinely pleased, not seeming to think it odd that women's jewelry had found a home amidst hunting and camping gear.

"Sawyer Banks—he's the owner—gave me the names of a few other shop owners he thinks might be interested in carrying jewelry, as well." One was a tack shop. The other a bait and tackle. But beggars couldn't be choosers, right?

Luke set the bin back down on the table. "It sounds as if doors are opening. Are you working on anything new? If you're starting to sell, you don't want to deplete your stock."

She shrugged, knowing he was right but not quite willing to pull out her tools of the trade again. Just the thought of it turned loose a bucketful of butterflies in her stomach. "Like I told you before, I have other priorities for the summer. But I'm young. There's plenty of time for such as that later."

She stood, fishing in her jacket pocket for car keys. He hoisted the bin again, the gaze directed at her touched once more with the sadness she hated to see there.

"Time flies fast, Delaney. Don't wait too long."

Who was he to be giving advice?

Sure, she'd given him some, but this was different. Luke gripped the bin more tightly as Delaney disappeared around the side of the inn. Despite her allusions to needed areas of growth, he was doing okay raising his kids. Even she admitted that. And yeah, maybe he'd come across as a bit of an arrogant know-it-all about parenting when some of her comments had hit too close to home.

But the elusiveness of time? The necessity of living each day deliberately? That's something he knew about, having learned the hard way by letting hours, days, months and years slip by for much too long. He was doing something about that now, though, wasn't he? Taking charge for a change with a relocation to Kansas?

He moved slowly toward the back of the inn, knowing that the moment he set foot inside he'd have to provide an explanation for muffling Chloe's teary outburst. He could have done without Delaney's reminder of her youth, of the decade yawning between them. How, though, could he make her see that time was finite and unpredictable?

There had been a lot of things he once thought he'd have more than enough opportunity for. Building a military career. A home life. Friends. Family. Fun. A deeper walk with God.

Time to be the kind of husband God had intended him to be.

But time could easily get away from you, slip through your fingers, and suddenly the opportunities were no more.

In her rearview mirror, Delaney could see the arching gateway to Hunter's Hideaway, then a curve through the pines ended that final glimpse leading to the home of a family she'd already found herself getting attached to.

Was Luke right? Did her encouraging words regarding Anna's creative gifts apply equally to her?

And why should he care?

Dwayne hadn't. Yet her own words practically

echoed her old boyfriend about there being plenty of time later to indulge her "little hobby."

From the look on Luke's face, he'd obviously disagree with Dwayne and Aunt Jen's assessment. Yet he'd been evasive when she'd asked him what dream he personally held, pointing nobly to his family's health and happiness. Yes, those were worthwhile dreams. But surely he had a dream for himself, didn't he? Maybe a special talent he longed to fulfill. Something God had placed in his heart that wouldn't go away. Is that why he wanted to leave Hunter Ridge?

"Doesn't he ever get lonely, Lord?" she said aloud, a hint of petulance in her tone that even she recognized. "Doesn't he ever dream of finding another wife to share his life with?"

She huffed an exasperated sigh as she rolled down the window, the sound of gravel crunching soothingly under the tires. Luke was a nice guy. With the coolest family. She couldn't imagine why he wanted to move away from them.

She'd give almost anything to have a big extended family like his. To live in the rustic charm of Hunter's Hideaway, a place where he had deep, deep roots to ground him. God had blessed her with an aunt and uncle who'd taken her in when she had nowhere else to go. Aunt Jen was kind and self-sacrificing, and did her best to see to Delaney's material needs. But the two of them had never been close.

Is that why today, in such a short time, she'd felt such a sense of belonging? Why she'd warmed instantly to Luke's family? The almost aristocratic Grandma Jo. The huggable Elaine and Luke's father, Dave. Good-humored Grady and spunky Rio. Undoubtedly, though, they'd extended hospitality to her as they would to any paying customer who crossed their threshold. That was their job, wasn't it? They earned their living making people feel welcome, yet she'd lapped it up like a thirsty pup.

At the absurdity of it, Delaney laughed aloud. All it had taken was a few hours among the Hunters and she'd not only decided Luke needed a wife, but she'd picked out her future in-laws, as well.

Chapter Fifteen

"She's a lovely girl, isn't she?"

"Don't go there, Grandma." Luke didn't look up at the woman standing in the open doorway of his small Hunter's Hideaway office. Instead, he focused more intently on the computer screen in front of him.

He didn't need to ask who his grandmother was talking about. Even four hours after Delaney had left for town and he'd let his dismayed mother and grandmother in on his plans for relocation, his head was still filled with images of the flirtatious sparkle in Delaney's eyes. The sound of her laughter. Her concern for him and his children.

"Your kids like her. She likes them, too."

He lifted a shoulder. "She seems to."

"Chloe says she likes you, as well."

"What's not to like?" He tapped at the keyboard with renewed determination, ignoring the unexpected warmth flooding through him at his grandmother's observations.

Josephine Hunter moved to the side of his desk, her well-manicured fingers pushing the laptop's cover forward so he could no longer see the screen. "It's been six years, Luke."

He shoved back in his chair and lifted his gaze to the woman looking down at him with equal parts compassion and fire in her eyes.

"Six years and three months, Grandma." Time was strange. In many ways that heartrending season of his life seemed long ago, as if it had happened to someone else. Yet, in other ways, Marsha's departure felt as raw as yesterday.

"It was not your fault."

Wasn't it? Maybe if he'd left the military sooner, spent more time with her. Been a better husband. Prayed harder.

Grandma propped her hip on the edge of the desk. "I know exactly what's going through your head. All the what-ifs and maybe-I-should-haves. I went through that when your grandfather died, certain I could have made him take the heart disease diagnosis more seriously. Made him slow down, get further medical treatment. But you know what?"

It wasn't as if they hadn't been over this ground before. "Yeah, you married a stubborn old coot."

She nodded briskly. "Exactly. I had to come to terms with the fact that as much as I'd like to, I can't control everything and everyone around me. You have that streak in you, too, Luke. But sometimes it doesn't serve either of us well."

He stared at her in silence, knowing how much

she missed Grandpa Ben. How her world had been yanked out from under her when that second heart attack proved fatal. But his grandpa hadn't *chosen* to leave Grandma any more than she would have chosen to leave him.

Marsha had made a decision.

Grandma reached over to pat his clenched fist resting on the desktop. "Why can't you give Delaney a chance? God's dropped this lively young lady right into your life."

"She's lively all right. And definitely young. Real young."

"So?" A smile twitched as she assessed him. "You have a few more good miles left in you."

That brought forth a reluctant smile that he quickly suppressed. "Ten years is a big gap. She has her whole life ahead of her. I've probably lived almost half of mine. I've already done the career thing. The parenting thing." The failing a spouse thing. "Do you realize she's as close to Travis's age as she is to mine? I sure don't need to take on another kid to raise."

Grandma frowned. "Is that how you see her? As another kid?"

No, not really. But he didn't intend to share how he did see her. Those lovely eyes. A radiant smile. A laugh that made him want to laugh, too. "She has a lot of growing up to do."

Grandma snorted. "And you don't?"

"She's impulsive, doesn't always think things

through. She's bitten off more than she can chew on this youth group project. A house that, as you know, is intended for Benton Mason and his family."

"You haven't joined the others at the project house today. Do you intend to?"

Somebody needed to keep an eye on things, make sure Delaney didn't get carried away in her well-intentioned but naive endeavors. "I get the impression I'm not wanted there."

"By whom?"

"My son. My daughter. Delaney."

"On the contrary, I'm under the impression that Delaney does want you there. It would give you more time to get to know each other."

He leaned forward. "Grandma, haven't you heard a word I've said? Delaney's a nice young woman. I'm not arguing that. I'm saying we're worlds apart and I think neither you nor I would argue that I already learned the lesson behind a similar reality the hard way. Besides, I think Garrett has his eye on her and I'm not getting in the middle of that."

No way would he make a fool of himself competing with his much younger cousin for Delaney's attention.

"What makes you think he's interested in her?"

"He's brought up her name in every conversation I've had with him in the past few weeks. That's what Anna and Travis have always done when they're infatuated with someone. He seems to be over at the project house or nagging me to work on it to help her every time I turn around."

"But he hasn't said anything to you about it?"

Luke hiked a brow. "I'm not his confidant."

"Well, I think you're wrong about him," she stated, the exasperation in her voice coming through loud and clear. "Can't you see, Luke? You're a good man who got knocked to his knees by an undeserved tragedy. You're a responsible parent who puts far more effort into those relationships than most. A hard worker who seldom gives himself a break. What's wrong with doing something nice for yourself for a change—such as enjoying the company of a woman like Delaney Marks?"

"Grandma—"

"You've been running scared, Luke. Now you're pulling up stakes and dragging your kids off with you. What do you think will be any different in Kansas? What makes you think you can get away from all that haunts you here when those very things are buried deep down inside?" She clutched her fist to her heart. "You'll only pack them up and take them with you."

She stood looking down at him for a long moment, the love in her eyes willing him to listen, to act. Then with a brisk nod, she left him alone in the room.

"Nobody gets it, Lord," he mumbled under his

breath as he turned to stare out the window. Not even Grandma. Couldn't anyone see it wasn't about what was best for him—what he needed, what he wanted and desired—but about what was best for his kids?

And what was best for any misguided woman who attempted to take up with him.

Dare she tell Luke?

Although Delaney had thought endlessly about the things he'd said as they sat at the Hunter's Hideaway picnic table last weekend, prayed about the situation and finally stepped out in faith, he wasn't going to like this.

She looked down at the cream-colored business card in her hand. *Benton Mason. Artist.*

When she'd garnered the courage earlier that morning to return to the Artists' Co-op to take Sunshine up on her offer for assistance, she hadn't expected to meet right then and there the father of the family for which they were fixing up the house. And she certainly hadn't anticipated one of the bearded man's areas of expertise would be silverwork.

With only a moment's prayerful hesitation, she'd signed on, trusting that Sunshine wouldn't set her up with him if she didn't think he'd be a reliable and capable instructor. His jewelry on display at the Co-op proved he'd made the jury's selective cut, didn't it? Now she was over-the-top excited.

But knowing how Luke felt about the Masons…

"Hey, anybody home?"

At the sound of Luke's voice, she tucked the card into the side pocket of her purse and returned the bag to the kitchen countertop. No, he wasn't going to like this one bit.

"Back here!" As always, her spirits lifted at the sound of his voice. She hadn't seen him for days. He hadn't joined them for the amazingly productive work day after the trail ride. Then she'd gone to church in Canyon Springs on Sunday morning to see her aunt and, surprisingly, he hadn't shown up for youth group that night. Was that a sign that he'd taken into consideration her plea to give Travis and Anna some breathing room?

He stepped into the kitchen and set a red metal toolbox on the counter next to her purse, then surveyed the space in that now-familiar hands-on-his-hips stance. Did he have any idea how manly—and bossy—that made him look?

"I see that the scaffolding outside has been taken down. The painters are finished?"

"They wrapped it up yesterday afternoon."

"Good thing." He nodded toward a curtain-less window at the darkening sky. "Looks like we could see some monsoon rains this afternoon."

"It does." She motioned toward the house at

large. "It's not just the painters making progress, though. The boys and Anna had a grand time on Saturday ripping out old carpet down here. The others started stripping wallpaper. But that's going to take longer than anticipated." She rolled her eyes, tamping down a ripple of worry. "*All* the rooms are papered."

"One step at a time. I thought I'd come by and measure the floors where you want to replace linoleum. Too bad it was laid directly on concrete, but this room already looks amazing. It's really come together."

"It has. I think we'll go with tile in here and in the bathrooms. The hardwood floors under the carpet in the living and dining rooms are in surprisingly good condition. The upstairs carpets just require a good professional cleaning, but I won't schedule that until we get the walls finished."

Gazing around the kitchen at its sparkling white cabinetry and creamy yellow walls, Delaney's memory leaped immediately to the meals shared around a kitchen table with her own family. Mom. Dad. Grandma. Tiffany. Close times of love and laughter. No amount of wishful thinking could bring back those days, but could she make a way for another family to create their own precious memories?

"Delaney?"

Startled back to the present, an ache still lingering in her heart, visions of her family evaporated. She turned to Luke. "Sorry. I was in my own little world there for a minute."

"I could tell." His eyes held a curious light but, thankfully, he didn't pry. "I was saying I hope the kids can get farther along on the wallpaper so you can start the painting sooner than later. We're not that far from move-in day."

He didn't need to remind her. Even though she'd been warned, she'd underestimated the hours that the kids would be working jobs, taking vacations and participating in other activities. Next weekend was Paris and Cody's wedding so she'd be gone all day, too. She was determined to trust God, not to panic, but the approaching deadline had cost her more than a few nights' sleep.

Luke opened his toolbox and snagged a hefty-looking tape measure, but as he turned his elbow caught the edge of her purse, knocking it to the floor.

"Sorry." He quickly stooped to retrieve her bag, then popped it back on the countertop. "I hope I didn't break anything."

"Nothing to break." Her cell phone was well-buried in its depths.

He handed her the body of the tape measure while he held on to the metal end of the tape, instructing her to move to the far side of the room. He knelt down, preparing to place it on the floor next to the wall behind him. Then paused to pick up something from the floor.

A cream-colored card.

Luke turned the card over, thinking that he must have knocked the home improvement clerk's contact card out of his toolbox. But it didn't belong to him.

He looked up at Delaney. What was she doing with Benton Mason's business card? He stood and held it out to her. "This must have fallen out of your purse."

She came forward, allowing the tape measure to reel back in, then plucked the card from his fingers. But she didn't meet his gaze. "Thanks."

"Did his wife give that to you?"

She handed him the tape measure, glanced down at the card, and then tucked it away in her purse. "No, actually Sunshine Carston gave it to me."

"How come?"

"He makes jewelry."

"You intend to buy some of his stuff?"

"No."

What was this, a game of twenty questions? "I'm not saying it's a crime to have his business card. I was curious as to why Sunshine would give it to you."

She leaned back against the counter, her hands gripping the edges on either side of her, then met his questioning gaze with an uncertain one of her own. "You're the one who told me I shouldn't give up on my dreams."

"Right."

"When I first met Sunshine, she suggested that my next step might be apprenticing under a mentor. But feeling like I'd been kicked in the teeth at the Co-op's rejection, I'd turned down her offer to help me find someone."

He didn't like where this was going.

She offered an uncertain smile. "You—and that conversation about Anna's poetry—convinced me to change my mind."

"Benton Mason is going to be your mentor?" What was Sunshine thinking, setting Delaney up with him? He still couldn't believe Dad and Grady had decided to hire him part-time.

She gave a quick nod, excitement lighting her eyes. "Tomorrow's my first lesson."

For a long moment he stood speechless. How could he get her to see that this was a bad idea? "Look, Delaney, I know this is none of my business—"

"You're right," she said almost cheerfully. "It's not."

He paused, digesting her quick response. "You don't know the story behind the Masons. I wouldn't advise—"

"It's already settled. Sunshine had earlier arranged studio space and a room at the co-op for him and Drake to stay until the house is done. That's why we've seen his son around. To pay for my lessons I'll work in the gallery to fill in for him when he can't meet his Co-op volunteer obligations."

"He's dumping his responsibilities on you?"

"It's only a handful of weekly hours. I suspect he has rehabilitation out of town, so he'll only be here a few days a week. But we need to get this place fixed up by the deadline so his family can be under one roof again."

Delaney seemed more than determined to make that happen, not even considering that the family might be better off without Benton. Or at least better off moving to a more affordable community and getting real jobs like regular people.

"If he's back in town even part-time, it seems to me he should be the one over here getting this place in shape. Not giving art lessons and making you and a group of high school kids do the dirty work."

For a moment, his words hung, supercharged, between them.

Then, eyes narrowed, Delaney's words came softly. "For whatever reason, Luke, you've let the Masons get under your skin, haven't you? You may want to consider showing more compassion for a family experiencing some hard times."

She was reprimanding him based on perceptions of Benton Mason's hard times? He could tell her about hard times ten times over. But he'd long ago resolved not to play the pity card.

"You might," he said slowly, "feel less kindly toward them if you knew that ninety-percent of their so-called problems are of their own making."

Her gaze didn't waver. "Isn't that the truth for all of us?"

As her words sunk in, an invisible vise tightened around his chest. Believing that, if she knew of his situation she'd undoubtedly assume he'd brought down on himself and his family the hardships of the past six years.

And, despite Grandma's insistence to the contrary, very likely he had.

Chapter Sixteen

Delaney stood, frozen, staring into Luke's stricken eyes. Why had she made that insensitive comment? How could she have forgotten, even momentarily, that Luke's wife had killed herself? That survivor's guilt would naturally haunt him?

An almost uncontrollable urge to slip her arms around him and beg his forgiveness shot through her. But what explanation could she offer for such brazen behavior? He didn't know she knew the truth of his tragic loss and any attempt to apologize for her thoughtless words would have to touch on that. Which was exactly the thing Garrett had warned her not to do.

The doorbell echoed loudly through the empty house, a death knell on the opportunity to make things right with Luke.

"Anybody around?" a hearty male voice called through the screen door.

"Kitchen countertop installation," she moaned. She'd forgotten workmen were coming from the home improvement store in Canyon Springs. So much was going on that she'd gotten mixed up on her days. Torn, Delaney hesitated, loath to leave her conversation with Luke hanging, but he motioned her forward.

The installer didn't have good news. When he'd gone to unload the countertops, he discovered a worker had packed the van with the wrong order. A call back to the store confirmed hers hadn't arrived yet after all. In fact, there had been a mix-up and it would be delayed.

When the apologetic installer left, Delaney couldn't stifle a giggle as she turned to the handsome man standing in the middle of the living room floor. It was either laugh or cry.

"What's so funny?"

"A week's delay. That's on top of discovering this morning that the gallons of paint I picked up yesterday—a special mix—are the wrong color and I'll have to drive to Canyon Springs to take them back. And the guys who are to put in the new fence can't schedule it in until the week of our deadline. And—"

"I think you need to give it up, Delaney."

She laughed. But he wasn't smiling. Her smile faded, too. "You're not serious."

"I am. You're knocking yourself out on this project and every time you turn around something goes wrong. Doesn't that tell you something?"

"You mean every time a goal is challenged, you'd advise throwing in the towel? Is that what you tell your kids?"

"That's not what I'm saying."

"I don't understand, then. What *are* you saying?"

"You're running out of time here. The kids are starting to feel pressured. Their summer is slipping away. This was supposed to be a part-time volunteer job for you, too, remember?"

"I admit I'd hoped for more free time, but the primary reason I'm in Hunter Ridge is to provide support for the youth group and for this project in particular."

"Nobody would fault you for saying, 'Hey, with the setbacks we've encountered—the asbestos scare, the rain, the delays—it's not going to happen.' I'm not saying not to follow through, but maybe that early-finish bonus just isn't realistic. It's out of your control."

"Being in control is the most important thing to you, isn't it?" It seemed to be his all-driving force. "You need to loosen up, Luke."

"And you, Delaney…" Luke's brow furrowed as he weighed his words. "Need to get your feet back on the ground. You've let your Pollyanna outlook affect your better judgment when it comes to this project. You've known all along the deadline is tight."

"Luke—" But despite the protest forming on her lips, the truth of his words pierced. Deep. She'd ignored nagging doubts, focused on the positive. Refused to listen to anything contrary to her hopes. Her throat tightened. *She wasn't going to make the deadline.* And no amount of optimism or personal effort was going to change that. She'd run out of time.

"It doesn't matter how much you and the kids put into this," Luke continued, his tone now coaxing as if recognizing in her eyes that reality was hitting home. "The bonus will be lost, so why not back off and give yourself and the kids an additional four weeks? Or better yet, admit you've done all you and the youth group can do and let High Country Hope recruit other volunteers to finish things up. Putting any more time in on this will only be in vain."

But she desperately wanted the youth group to receive the bonus. They'd worked hard and had plans to meet with Garrett and the church board to present ideas on how to spend it. Amazingly unselfish ideas. And most of all, she wanted the Masons—especially little Samantha—to have a home sooner rather than later.

She'd only met the girl once. But somehow she'd become the heart and soul of this project. Like family.

"No, it's not in vain," she said quietly, as renewed determination rose in her. "Samantha Mason *will* have her family living together by the end of July even if…if it's the last thing I do."

Her fingers fisted at her sides as tears pricked her eyes.

Luke stepped closer, his concerned gaze searching hers. "Why's getting Samantha's family back together so important to you?"

"Because families deserve to be together." Her lower lip quivered. "Just as my family deserved to be together. But we aren't. We can't be."

Confusion filled his eyes. "I don't understand."

As she tried to regain control, memories of those she'd loved most flashed through her mind. *Please, God. Let him understand.* "My grandma, my parents—and my little sister—were killed in a car accident when I was fourteen."

Surprise flashed in Luke's eyes, but she rushed on. "That's why I moved to Canyon Springs to live with my aunt Jen. My sister was only twelve, Luke. The same age as Samantha. Samantha even reminds me of her in more ways than I can count. There's nothing I can do to bring my family back again. But I can give Samantha's family a second chance."

Heart aching, Luke stared into the eyes of the beautiful, hurting woman before him. "I didn't know, Delaney. I'm sorry. I had no idea."

She blinked rapidly, her fists still clenched. "You wouldn't. Couldn't. I didn't tell you."

"Why not?" There had been many opportunities when she could have explained why this project was so important to her. When she could have enlightened him rather than leaving him with the impression that her deciding on the Mason house project was an ill-thought-out whim. But she hadn't.

She pressed her lips together, as if gathering energy for her next words. "I know it may sound silly to you, but I've had to live with that burden, that shadow of loss since I was a teen. With having my aunt introduce me to people with a somber aside—'Her parents were killed in a car accident, you know. Her grandma and sister, too.' It was repeated so often, that it formed my identity, became how people related to me."

She clenched her fingers even tighter. "I was hurting inside, but I didn't want to be an object of pity. So I didn't talk about it. I didn't want strangers prying into my pain uninvited."

So she thought of him as a stranger? The ache in his chest increased.

"But can't you see now why keeping this family together is important to me, Luke? My family was splintered apart. I can't bring them back. But I'll do almost anything to do that for this family— for Samantha." She drew a deep breath, her gaze piercing into his. "And I won't let you or anyone else stop me."

He stared into the resolve sparking in her eyes, then down at those determined fists. Like him, she'd suffered unspeakable loss. Buried the anger. But where he'd withdrawn from life, purposefully focused on his children to the exclusion of all other things, she'd opened her heart to others. Like the Masons.

Reaching for one of her hands, he raised it to hold in both of his. Warm and fragile, yet at the same time remarkably strong. Like Delaney. Tenderly he unfurled each tightly clamped finger. The hand of an artist. The hand that sought to give a family the second chance she'd never get. He silently traced his finger along her palm, her citrusy scent filling his senses. Then with a shaky breath he raised his eyes to look at her. "I won't stand in your way, Delaney. I promise."

She blinked back tears, her hopeful gaze searching his as if for confirmation. His beautiful Delaney. A woman with a sensitive heart and gentle eyes that saw the hurts of the world and wanted to heal them.

"Luke…"

Releasing her hand, he placed a silencing finger to her mouth. And then, as if it were the most natural thing in the world, he leaned in to brush his lips against hers.

Soft. Sweet.

He caught the sound of her quick intake of breath, then his heart swelled as her arms hesitantly encircled his neck. He drew slightly back and for a long moment they stared into each other's eyes. Those big beautiful Delaney eyes he'd come to…love?

He swallowed. Then buried a hand in that silky

softness of her hair—and lowered his mouth once again to hers. As he deepened the kiss, feelings he'd too long denied crashed through him like waves upon a rocky shore. Powerful. Inevitable. So right. How could he not have seen it coming?

Delaney. His Delaney. He slipped his arms around her, pushing aside the protest his mind clamored to force to the surface. He didn't want to think about the past. The future. He wanted only to savor now. This moment. The woman in his arms.

And yet… *What now, God?*

A flash of lightning and the rumble of thunder brought them reluctantly back to reality, the scent of rain now strong on the cool breeze that forced its way through the open screen door.

Delaney drew slightly back, breathless, her eyes questioning. "I didn't expect that."

He leaned his forehead against hers, loath to let her go. "Me, neither."

For several silent minutes they stood, arms entwined. Were a million unanswered questions pelting through her mind as they were his? How he wanted to make things right for her. To protect her, keep her safe. To have her be a part of his life.

But how was that even possible? A weight settled into his chest. "We'll get this house done by the deadline. Whatever it takes."

She looked up at him. "Do you think we can?"

He nodded. "We'll give Samantha a house. But then…"

"Then what?"

"Then it's up to her parents to give her a home. Or not. That's one thing neither of us can control. You can't take on the burden of ownership for that, Delaney. But we can help them open a door to a second chance. It's up to them whether or not they walk through it."

"Thank you, Luke." An impish smile surfaced. "See? You *are* a superhero just like you always wanted to be."

Yeah, right. Like he believed that. But nevertheless, he kissed her forehead, cherishing these moments of closeness. How long it had been since he'd held a woman in his arms. Felt a connection. A bond. Love? He'd committed to helping Delaney and he would. He'd do everything within his power to bring her dream for the Masons to pass.

But anything else?

No, he wasn't the man she thought him to be. No superhero by a long shot. He hadn't been strong enough, faith-filled enough, to stop his wife from harming herself and shattering his children's lives.

How could he risk breaking another woman's heart, too?

"He *kissed* you days ago and I'm not hearing about it until now?"

Paris, breathtaking in a simple, floor-length white lace dress, turned from the mirror at Canyon Springs Christian Church on Saturday afternoon to face Delaney. Her voice took on a lightly scolding tone. "So why isn't he here with you at my wedding? I put 'and guest' on the invitation, didn't I?"

"I think a first date at a wedding is too much pressure on both of us. I wouldn't want my friends overwhelming him. Making assumptions. It's not like we're engaged." In fact, she wasn't quite sure what they were. But God knew, right? That's what counted.

"Yeah, our friends might be a bit much. But when Cody and I get back from our honeymoon, we'll invite the two of you to dinner. Promise you'll get Luke there?"

"Promise."

Throughout the ceremony and on into the reception, Delaney could hardly keep her mind on her maid-of-honor duties. When her best friend and the handsome groom had sealed their vows with a kiss, it was all she could do not to put her fingertips to her own lips and relive every precious moment of Luke's unexpected embrace.

While standing in the Mason house living room—broad daylight in the middle of a workweek—hadn't been the most romantic setting for a first kiss, somehow it seemed appropriate considering the project had brought them together. No, there had been no promises or even hints of promises, but he had vowed to help her make the deadline. Knowing how Luke felt about the Masons, that was as good as a commitment, wasn't it?

Still bubbling over with wonder at how their relationship had taken such an amazing turn, following the wedding she'd spent the night at her aunt's in Canyon Springs and gone to church there in the morning. There was evidence upon her return to Hunter Ridge that Luke had overseen the workday in her absence as promised. But, to her disappointment, he hadn't put in an appearance at the youth group meeting Sunday evening or at the Mason house when she'd been there. Just like the fabled elf who came in the night to assist a shoemaker, he'd obviously been there before she arrived or after she left.

"But it's Monday, Lord," she said aloud as she selected a few pieces of jewelry from her earlier efforts to drop off at the Echo Ridge Outpost. "Five days after that amazing kiss, and not even a phone call."

How tempting it was to call him. But maybe he needed time to pray about their relationship, to contemplate where it might be headed. He had children to consider, too. Nevertheless, it took every ounce of self-control not to let her imagination run far ahead of where they actually were—to wedding bells and motherhood and happily-ever-after.

The sobering truth, however, was that they had a major hurdle to overcome, for not once had he shared more than a quick reference to his wife's death. Nothing about the impact or circumstances surrounding it. And no words of...love.

She'd just be patient. Or try to be.

A merry tune suddenly played from the recesses of her purse. She dug frantically around in the bag, then snatched up her phone. *Please, please, let it be Luke.*

But the caller ID was one she hadn't seen since May.

Her former employer.

"So when are you going to ask Delaney out?" Rio cast Luke a sideways glance as she placed a plate of fresh-baked cookies on the table of his cabin kitchen. Killer chocolate chip. That was Rio's only claim to domestic fame.

"I think," she added, seating herself in the chair across from him and snagging a cookie, "Grady's ready to make a move if you don't hurry it up."

Little did his siblings know that he'd already made a move. One that knocked his world right off its axis. But as sweet as those moments holding Delaney in his arms had been, he'd had no business kissing her. Leading her on. Thankfully, he'd had the presence of mind not to talk of love. So there would be no expectations, would there?

The thought of Grady—of any man—moving in on Delaney, though, didn't set right with him, either. "Tell him he'd better clear it with Garrett first."

But would Delaney have kissed Luke the way she did if she had any interest in his cousin?

Rio waved a cookie at him. "Grandma Jo asked me if I knew anything about that, so I just flat-out asked Garrett last night. He's proclaiming his innocence. In fact—" her tone held a teasing lilt "—he claims he's done about everything he can to get you two together."

"What?"

"He says he was afraid he'd never be able to convince you he couldn't figure out how to plug in a microwave. But you fell for it and came running to Delaney's rescue."

Luke frowned, recalling the incident, but Rio's grin lured out a smile of his own.

"Brat."

"Me or Garrett?" Rio broke off a piece of cookie and tossed it at him. He caught it midair and popped it in his mouth.

"The both of you."

"Honestly, Luke, everybody thought for sure that after the two of you sat out at the picnic table talking after everyone left that day, that we'd hear you'd asked her out. Cold feet?"

"Common sense." But it had been days since he'd spoken with her, had promised he'd see that she made that deadline. He couldn't keep going in at odd hours to work on the project house. No, a better route would be to show up when kids and other parents were around. Make it easier for them both.

"Luke?" Rio pitched another chunk of cookie at him. He missed and it hit the floor. "The whole family agrees. Don't let her get away."

They wanted her back in Sacramento. At a higher salary. And, if she agreed to return by the first week of August, an office with a window.

With Luke's kiss fresh in her mind, however, her first instinct had been to say no. But now, a few days later, she was glad she hadn't been so hasty. Had asked for time to think about it.

"He's alone in what's going to be Samantha's room," Travis whispered to her. "Now might be a good time."

Earlier that morning Anna and Travis had quietly approached her at the Mason house, asking that she talk to Luke regarding the move to Kansas. To be their advocate. They said he'd listen to her. That he'd respect her opinion. She might possibly have agreed a week ago, but now? Had they not noticed the tension between them whenever she and Luke were in the same room?

"I know I said I'd think about it, Trav, but I doubt it will do any good. Your father's mind is made up."

"Please?"

How could she turn down those pleading eyes,

so clear and blue and earnest? So much like his father's.

This was probably going to be a mistake, but for the kids' sake, she had to try, didn't she? "Okay. But don't get your hopes up."

He gave her a thumbs-up and cut a glance at Anna, who flashed a hopeful smile.

Knowing how rare moments alone with Luke had been—as in nonexistent—she nevertheless stopped to praise the painting going on in the dining room and the final stripping of wallpaper in the entry. Then, with purposeful steps, she climbed the staircase to the second floor.

The day following the job offer, Luke had appeared at the house as if no time had passed—and no kiss had taken place. He'd greeted her warmly, then set to work alongside the pack of kids and several parents who'd accompanied him. She'd waited restlessly, hopefully, all day, eager for a moment to finally have a word in private. But the brief snatches of time were filled only with talk of the project. And as the days stretched out, it was clear that her fears had been realized. He regretted the kiss. Chose to pretend it had never happened.

Delaney paused in the hallway outside Samantha's room, briefly closing her eyes for a quick prayer. *Here goes, Lord.* She opened her eyes just in time to jump back as Luke strode out of the bedroom.

He jerked to a halt. "Sorry. Didn't see you there."

For a moment their eyes met and she recognized in his the same uncertain awareness she'd felt in his presence in recent days. But how handsome he looked today, wearing that shade of blue that brought out the color of his eyes.

He looked down at her, his expression now friendly enough, yet impersonal. "Is there something I can help you with?"

"Do you have a few minutes?"

His expression once again flashed to uncertainty, a wariness almost, that made her stomach churn uncomfortably. Why had she promised Travis she'd do this?

"It's about your kids," she quickly added before Luke could find an excuse to dash off.

He frowned. "Is there a problem?"

She glanced back down the stairs where Kendrick and Sybil were stripping wallpaper. "Not exactly. But can I speak to you in private for a moment?"

He hesitated, then stepped back and motioned her into Samantha's room where, from the looks of things, he'd been putting up curtain rods.

"So what's up?"

She strolled over to the window to look out on the yard they'd worked so hard on. Then turned again to Luke. "First off, you have every right to tell me this is none of my business."

His brows raised. "Can't say I like the sound of that."

"But I ask that you nevertheless hear me out." She sounded so prim, so businesslike, when all she wanted to do was slip into his arms, place her head on his chest and ask him to hold her close. "Are you willing to do that?"

"If it involves my kids, I guess I have no choice."

"I'm here on behalf of Anna and Travis and— indirectly—Chloe." He didn't interrupt, so she continued. "They asked me to talk to you. About the move to Kansas."

He chuckled. "Believe me, Delaney, I've heard it all."

She took a step toward him, willing him not to shut her out. "Maybe you've *heard* it, but have you *understood* it? Hearing with your ears and understanding with your heart are two different things."

His gaze sharpened. "So my kids are confiding in you, now?"

"I'm not soliciting it, if that's what you're thinking. But I did tell them I'd speak to you. Maybe I could help them understand, if I understood the situation better myself."

He didn't answer immediately, instead studying her a long moment. Then nodded. "Okay. It's like this. After my wife died, I left the army and brought the kids back here. My family generously offered me a job keeping the books for Hunter Enterprises. Am I clear so far?"

She nodded, sensing his irritation with having to explain this to her.

"Living here, there are limited opportunities. No future here for my children. An opportunity has presented itself in Kansas. End of story."

But somehow she sensed it wasn't, and bits and pieces she'd picked up from earlier conversations suddenly came together, like metal filings to a magnet.

"You don't enjoy your job here, do you?"

Surprise lit his eyes. "What gives you that idea?"

"Things you've said. About it not being your dream job. How you resent Benton Mason for pursuing his, when you're only doing yours because it 'needs to be done' and provides for your family."

"You're too perceptive for your own good."

"Have you talked to your family about this, Luke? About your dissatisfaction with your job? Maybe some adjustments can be made."

"Nice thought, Delaney, but it won't happen. I walked out on Hunter Enterprises when I was eighteen years old. Big showdown with Dad. Joined the army. Now my younger brother Grady is living the future I turned my back on. I don't think my dad will ever forgive me." He drew a breath. "So now, if we've covered this topic to your satisfaction, I need to get downstairs and see about meeting a deadline."

* * *

Why'd he go and tell her all that?

But she needed to know that despite appearances to the contrary, the Hunters were like any other family on the face of the earth. Just people. People doing their best with what life had dealt them. Doing their best to get along. Looking to God to sustain them when the going got rough. But maybe now she could see why the opportunity his buddies in Kansas were giving him was one he couldn't pass up.

It was all he could do, though, when her eyes had pleaded for him not only to hear what his kids were saying but to *understand* them, not to pull her into his arms and demand that she understand him, too. But how could she? There was so much that she didn't know about him. That, God willing, she'd never know.

But he'd seen the hurt in her eyes when he'd abruptly brought their conversation to a halt. And his heart ached that he'd never know the sweet taste of her lips on his again.

Chapter Seventeen

Still shaken from their conversation, Delaney lingered in Samantha's room, gazing, unseeing, out the window.

Like two strangers, they'd stood in that very room as though in opposite corners of a boxing ring. If only there was a way to make things right for him. To heal the hurts of the past. Ease the pain of his wife's death and his estrangement with his father. His dissatisfaction with his job. His relationship with his children. It weighed heavily upon her, too, that there would be no future with Luke.

Not everyone is meant to be in your life forever.

That seemed to be the story of her life. Losing her grandmother, parents and sister. Her uncle. A serious boyfriend or two who'd come and gone. And now Luke.

But had she brought this on herself? Had trying to guard her heart against deeper hurt subconsciously sabotaged her relationship with Luke?

"He needs me, Lord," she whispered into the empty room.

He needs me.

She sighed, accepting God's truth. And yet… yesterday Sawyer Banks had let it slip that Luke had been responsible for getting her jewelry into the Outpost. Luke, who didn't have a whole lot of good to say about artists in this community, had done that for her. Why?

Before she made a final decision on the job offer, she had to know the answer to that question. And she had to know what, if anything, that kiss had meant to him. If he'd initiated a kiss, sensing God's leading, why had he then slammed the door in her—and God's—face?

Even if she had to swallow her pride, she needed answers. And she needed them now.

"Luke?"

He tensed at the sound of Delaney's voice carrying back to him in the kitchen. He thought she and the others had left for the evening. When she stepped through the arched doorway, he looked up from where he'd just finished laying another row of tile, drinking in the sight of her. A hesitant smile touching her lips, her presence always seemed to illuminate everything around her.

If only he could stop thinking about their kiss.

She knelt down to run her fingers along the smooth ceramic surfaces. "This looks great."

He nodded with a sense of satisfaction. But he couldn't let himself think about the fact that he was going to this effort for Benton Mason. No, not for Benton. For God.

And for Delaney.

She stood and leaned back against the counter. "You've been putting in an awful lot of time on this project, Luke."

"I told you we'd get 'er done, didn't I?" He smoothed a grout-filled seam with his thumb, then, standing, wiped it on the rag tucked in his belt. "But it does take time. Last I checked, this wasn't on any fairy godmother's to-do list."

She laughed softly. "I do have so much to thank you for. I understand you got Sawyer Banks to take my jewelry on consignment."

He'd told Sawyer to keep his mouth shut.

"You do a lot of nice things for me, Luke."

But never enough to make up to her the loss of her family. Never enough to make up for leading her on with that kiss. "It's my pleasure."

"Why?"

Caught off guard, he focused again on wiping his hands on the rag. "Why what?"

She pushed off from the counter, looking as light as a feather in her denim leggings, embroidered tunic and dainty sandals.

"Why is it a pleasure to help me? And..." She gazed at him almost helplessly, as if unsure of her next words. "What about that kiss?"

If the floor had given way under his feet, he couldn't have been more thunderstruck. He drew in a breath and let it out slowly. "Delaney, about that kiss…"

An amazing kiss. But he should have known he couldn't kiss her like that and not be called into account. How could he explain what she meant to him without her reading the wrong things into it?

Like a future that could never be.

"Did it mean anything to you at all?" She took a step toward him, her words coming softly, plaintively. Tearing a hole in his heart.

He hung his head for a long moment, unable to bear the brunt of her beautiful probing eyes. "More than you'll ever know."

Please don't let me hurt her, Lord.

He sensed her moving closer and took a step back before meeting her gaze. "Any man on earth would consider himself blessed to have you in his life. But as much as I wish it could be me, I'm not the man for you."

Her lower lip trembled. "I don't understand."

He moved to the back door to stand looking out at the last dregs of sunlight filtering through the pines. He didn't want to get into this, to see the stars fade from her eyes. But it had to be done.

"I wasn't a good husband, Delaney. God knows I tried, but it wasn't enough."

He pushed the screen door open and quickly stepped out onto the bricked patio, his gaze lifting to a sliver of moon. The scent of afternoon rain still hung delicately in the air.

Behind him he heard the screen door open, close, and knew she'd joined him.

"I'm sorry, Luke. So very sorry."

But she didn't know the half of it.

"Taking one's life…" she said softly, letting her words drift off.

He spun toward her. *She knew?* How? Had one of his kids…?

But did it really matter? The truth still had to come out. The truth he'd never told another living soul.

Delaney stared into Luke's pain-filled eyes. What a burden of guilt this man had borne the past six years. She should have seen that all along. Should've better understood how the tragedy impacted his relationship with his children. How it might affect his relationship with another woman.

But how could this loving, bighearted man blame himself for his wife's tragic mistake? "It's not your fault, Luke."

He avoided her gaze. "She chose to leave me."

"No, no, she didn't. She was ill. Very ill." She grasped his arms hanging woodenly at his sides. "Sometimes a mind can become sick, like any other organ in our body."

He turned away. "I know that intellectually. Just as I know God's forgiven me for any part I may have unknowingly played in her final decision. But in reality?" He drew a ragged breath. "I'm deeply ashamed that I couldn't have done more. Been more. Prayed more. So that my kids would still have their mother."

Her own heart ached at the shame he felt. The deep sense of failure weighing on a man who as a kid dreamed of being a superhero. The desperate need he must feel to make up the loss to his children.

"God loves you, Luke. He doesn't want you to bear this burden alone."

He hung his head and she longed to slip her arms around him. To comfort him. But he'd certainly pull away.

"I didn't realize at first what was happening. She'd always been moody, up one minute, down the next. Oddly enough, that had always been a part of her charm. Things were a bit rough after Chloe's birth, but she eventually bounced back. She was a good wife. A good mom. But after the accident…"

"Accident?"

He nodded. "She hit a little boy with her car. He just ran right out in the street in front of her. She was exonerated…but at the time they weren't sure if the kid would ever walk again. She was just sick about it. Couldn't get it out of her head."

"Understandably."

"I… I did my best to comfort her. To offer support. But sometimes—" He sighed heavily. "Sometimes when she'd wake up in the middle of the night, she couldn't get the accident out of her head, and she wouldn't even let me hold her."

Poor Luke.

"It wasn't until she was hospitalized for an overdose of pills that I recognized how serious the situation had become. I made sure she saw the right doctors. Got the right counselors. But it wasn't enough. *I* wasn't enough." He raked his fingers through his hair.

"Do you have any idea," he continued, his voice ragged, "what it's like to always be counting the pills in a medicine cabinet to see if any are missing? Living in fear when someone you love is even a few minutes late getting home from an errand? To see the confusion in your children's eyes when Mom locks herself in a darkened bedroom and won't come out for days?"

Delaney ran a comforting hand along his arm. He flinched, but didn't move away. *Please God, hold him close. Comfort him.*

He turned toward her, his eyes shadowed. "I'm sorry to dump this on you, Delaney, but there's something else you need to understand."

"It wasn't your fault, Luke."

"No?" He gave a harsh chuckle. "In all honesty, Delaney, those last months drained me. Mentally, emotionally, spiritually. I was running on nothing but fumes. Trying to meet my obligations at the army base. To see to Marsha's needs. To be mom and dad to three kids, the youngest barely out of diapers."

He gazed up at the moon, the shadows from the pine branches etching his face. "One day, far from the prying eyes of others, I finally broke down. Demanded from God to know why, if Marsha wanted to get away from me so badly…why didn't she get it over with and grant all of us merciful relief?"

Tears pricked Delaney's eyes. "Oh… Luke."

His jaw hardened, lost in the memories of that tragic time. "I was instantly appalled for thinking that, for having such little faith in God. I immediately asked forgiveness and set my heart on seeing the situation through, to be the rock my wife and kids needed me to be."

She reached out to take his hand. That big strong hand which had fought in wars and cradled his babies.

"Not too many days afterward…" He sucked in a breath, then slowly let it out. "I found her on the floor of the garage, the car engine running."

Delaney squeezed his hand as he swallowed hard, no doubt envisioning that horrifying scene.

"Thank God she'd dropped the kids off for a sleepover with friends. I'd gotten caught up in emergencies on the base, so was running late. I'd… I'd even stopped on the way home to pick up a bouquet of Marsha's favorite flowers."

He looked down at her, eyes bleak. "I've always

wondered, you know, if she sensed the desperation of that day when I'd broken down before God. When I'd as good as wished her dead and that's why—"

"Luke, *no*! Don't even think that."

"But now you can clearly see, Delaney, that I'm not the man you think I am." He grasped her by the arms and firmly set her aside. "I'm not the man for you, and I will never take another woman as my wife."

"I can't believe you're still planning to leave Hunter Ridge." Grady's accusing voice cut through the quiet of Luke's Hideaway office.

Moving away from the window, Luke met his brother's irritated gaze. "Believe it."

"You know it's going to kill Mom and Grandma Jo to see you and the kids leave. It's like a pall descended on this place ever since you made the announcement."

"Don't go thinking it was an easy decision to make. It wasn't. But it's time."

"Time for what? What can Kansas offer you that Hunter Ridge can't?"

Delaney wasn't there, for one thing. There'd been no sign of her at the project house today, the day after his confession. Had he so let her down that she couldn't even bear to see his face? But what could he expect, having bluntly told her how he'd faltered in his faith? That wasn't something that would endear him to many women, not even one as sweet-spirited as Delaney Marks.

A knot tightening in his stomach, Luke again faced the window to stare out at the property that in another month would no longer be his home.

When he'd walked away from her last night, heart aching and fearful of seeing the inevitable rejection in her eyes, she'd followed him to his truck. There she'd quietly informed him that she'd been offered a job with her former employer and would be leaving town at the end of the project.

No way did he believe Delaney wanted to return to that job in California. She'd dreamed of making a go of her jewelry-making talents, but that would take time and effort under the direction of a skilled mentor. Would she find someone like that elsewhere? Find the time out of her demanding workday to further pursue her dream? Returning to her old job was far from her heart's desire, but what alternative had he offered her?

In the span of six short years he'd managed to let down the two most important women in his life.

Good going, Hunter. Nice track record.

But he'd pushed himself hard, pressed the kids and other volunteers this week and they were almost done. They'd make that deadline for Delaney.

"Luke?" Grady punched him roughly in the shoulder. "Are you even listening to me? What can Kansas offer you that Hunter Ridge can't?"

Reluctantly, Luke turned to his brother. Maybe Delaney was right. He needed to come clean with the family.

"We skate around the truth, but we both know Dad's never forgiven me for not following in his footsteps." Luke motioned to his computer screen, the cursor on a payroll spreadsheet blinking in silent confirmation. "Get real, Grady. Bookkeeping isn't enough. Sure, I'm grateful to have had a job here. To have had family help me with the kids as I struggled to come to terms with Marsha's death. But there's no future for me here."

"You don't think so?"

"I know so."

"Then I think—" Grady leveled a determined gaze on him "—we'd better have a talk with Dad."

"Dad's letting me go on a camping trip with Nelson and Kendrick. And get this—he's not inviting himself along." Standing in a church hallway Sunday morning where he and Anna had caught Delaney for a whispered conversation, Travis fist-punched the air. "He's okayed my buying a truck, too."

Delaney couldn't help but smile at his excitement, marveling that Luke had encouraged his son to go on this adventure. But nevertheless, a ripple of apprehension touched her at the thought of the boys out in the wilderness on their own.

Suddenly she understood it hadn't been an easy decision for Luke to make.

"Honestly, I think Dad's going bonkers," Anna confided with a laugh. "Did you notice I'm wearing a bit of makeup this morning? And he said Chloe can go to a friend's sleepover."

"And best of all?" Travis leaned forward. "We're *not* moving to Kansas."

"You're not moving?" Delaney was stunned at Luke's one-eighty. "What happened?"

"Dad's worked out a deal with Grandpa and Uncle Grady to transition from bookkeeping into financial oversight. He's really stoked and so are they. He said he couldn't believe how close he came to making a big mistake."

It was evident that Luke's kids were thrilled by their dad's sudden transformation. But did it change anything for her?

"You'll be at the project house this afternoon, won't you, Delaney? For the dedication?" Anna looked at her hesitantly. "We've missed you."

"I've been there, behind the scenes." Anytime Luke's truck wasn't there. "I wouldn't miss the dedication for the world."

"Good. It wouldn't have happened without you. Without you and Dad, I mean."

Travis gave his sister a sharp look as if to silence her. What had Luke told them about their relationship? About her absence? Did they know she'd be leaving town soon?

"Delaney!" Surprised, she turned at the sound of her name, Anna and Travis scattering as a smiling Benton Mason approached, hand-in-hand with Samantha. How long had it been since the Masons had felt comfortable coming to church? "Sorry to interrupt, but I have to tell you that last night I saw the piece you're working on at the gallery studio. *Magnifico!*"

Her spirits rose at the unanticipated praise. Her lessons had been limited, but already she could see the wisdom of being under the tutelage of someone skilled in his craft. "That good?"

"Your best work in my humble opinion. If you keep this up, in a year or two the Co-op will be begging you to join."

Delaney's heart sank, but she kept her tone light. "Unfortunately, Benton, membership is only open to those living in Hunter Ridge or the surrounding area. I'll be leaving town in a few days."

"What?" His bushy brows lowered. "When did you intend to tell me about this?"

"The change in plans came up suddenly. A job offer that I can't turn down."

"I'm sorry to hear that. I'll miss our sessions. But if you keep honing your skills, someday you may be able to kiss that job goodbye."

He sounded sincere, and she knew that the opportunity to teach her his trade had increased his self-worth.

He shifted his gaze to his daughter, his expression softening, then focused again on Delaney. "I can't thank *you* enough for fixing up the house. For the prayers. A listening ear. Few people here in town know the whole story or would care to hear it even if they were given the opportunity. Which, I admit, I haven't given many. But thank you for a second chance."

He thrust his hand out for a shake, then thought better of it and pulled her into a quick embrace. "I wish you the best, Delaney."

"You, too, Benton."

She watched as her mentor—and how quickly he'd truly become one—again took his daughter's hand and headed toward the sanctuary.

"I couldn't help but overhear."

Delaney's heart leaped and she turned at the sound of Luke's voice as he stepped out from a side hallway.

"What," he continued, his gaze probing, "did Benton mean by 'the whole story'?"

Chapter Eighteen

Post-traumatic stress disorder.

Standing next to his truck at the project house that afternoon, Luke shook his head, remembering what the somber-eyed Delaney had reluctantly told him before hurrying off to the morning service. It wasn't her place to tell, she'd said somewhat tersely, avoiding eye contact as she made certain that no one else overheard them. Knowing how he felt about the Masons, though, she thought he needed to know.

After a few minutes, she was gone, leaving him standing alone in the empty hallway. He'd desperately wanted to reach out to her and—what? He had nothing to offer her that would banish the hurt from her eyes.

But Benton's PTSD? That explained a lot of things. The marriage difficulties. The drinking problem. Why he stayed closemouthed about his army background and didn't attempt to bond with others, like Luke, who'd shared similar experiences. Why he clung to the small town and to his art—both something he perceived as a less stressful means of supporting his family. How was it possible that in such a short time Delaney had learned what an entire town had failed to see?

Lesson learned, Lord. Not to judge so you won't be harshly judged yourself.

Luke secured his pickup's tool chest as the last car—except for Delaney's—pulled away. The dedication ceremony had been a moving one, with the youth group, extended Hunter family, and Benton and Lizzie and their children—including an appreciative Drake—present. Even Delaney's aunt, her friend Paris and several others from Canyon Springs had attended. Now it would no longer be a summer project but a family's new home, a place for a fresh start.

He turned to Travis, who was loading a ladder into the truck bed. "Where'd Delaney get off to?"

"She went back inside. She said she wanted to take one last look around before the Masons started moving stuff in. I think she intended to leave something special for Samantha." Travis peeled off his work gloves and tucked them in his belt. "Are you ready to leave now? I'd kind of like to run in and thank her. You know, for everything. She'll be gone by the time I get back from the camping trip."

Luke moved to the driver's door. He should probably say goodbye, too. Not leave that last strained conversation as their final memory. Then again, what else could be said? "Go ahead. Take your time. No hurry."

"Thanks." Travis gave him a hesitant smile. "You know, Dad, for a while there I thought…you know, that maybe you and Delaney…"

Travis's face reddened.

"As much as we all care for her, son, she has a life of her own to get back to."

"I know, but I bet she'd stay if you—"

Luke's heart hitched. "Don't go there, Travis. Some things aren't meant to be."

His son scuffed the toe of his boot in the gravel, looking as if he wanted to say more. Then he spun away and headed toward the house. With a weary shake of his head, Luke opened the truck door and slipped behind the wheel. A light breeze touched his cheek, and in the distance thunder rumbled, an apt accompaniment to the heaviness settling into his soul.

No, some things weren't meant to be.

"Dad!"

The fear in Travis's voice jerked his attention toward the house where his son stood just inside the open screen door, motioning wildly. In a flash, Luke leaped from the truck, his booted feet pounding up the drive.

Travis held the door open wider. "It's Delaney! I think she's unconscious!"

Heart racing, Luke bounded onto the porch,

pushing past his son and into the entry. "Where is she? Where—"

Bile rose in his throat at the sight of Delaney sprawled faceup on the living room floor, her golden hair spread out around her. Before he could stop it, the image of his nightmares hurtled him back in time.

Marsha. On the cold, concrete floor of the garage.

The remembered stench of car exhaust filled his nostrils. *Please, no, God. Please.*

"Dad?"

At the sound of Travis's voice he jerked back to the present, instantly dropping at Delaney's side to gently squeeze her shoulder. "Delaney, can you hear me?"

Receiving no response, he wove his fingers through the silky softness of her hair to the pulse point alongside her neck. A pulse. And she was breathing, her airway unblocked. No sign of blood. *Thank You, God.* Relief plowing through him, he nearly pulled her into his arms, but common sense reigned. Not knowing the injuries she may have sustained, he didn't dare move her.

"What...happened, Travis?" He could barely get the words out as he reached for her hand.

"I don't know. About the time I got to the front door, I heard a thud and something crash—probably that lamp—then found her like this."

Luke glanced around the partially furnished

room, registering a toppled floor lamp and a footstool which had skidded across the wooden floor to rest against the new rocker. Had she slipped and fallen? Fainted?

He thrust his cell phone at Travis who took it from him with shaking hands. "Call 911. Tell them she may have fallen. Hit her head. No known medical conditions."

"She's going to be okay, isn't she?" Travis's voice quavered as he punched in the number, then held the phone to his ear.

As his son reported Delaney's condition and location, Luke gently brushed her hair away from her face.

His beautiful Delaney.

Swallowing hard, he patted her hand. "Delaney?"

Please. Please, God. I can't lose another woman I love. Not Delaney. Not before…

A soft moan escaped her lips and she turned her head slightly.

He leaned in closer. "Don't move. You've hurt yourself."

Her eyelids flickered and he glanced back at Travis. "Tell them she may be regaining consciousness. Then throw me that afghan that's on the rocker."

"Rest easy there." He squeezed her hand. "Everything's going to be okay."

Her hand tightened on his as her confused eyes fluttered open.

"Luke?"

"Right here, babe." He took the afghan from Travis and with his free hand shook it open and tucked it in around her.

A faint smile touched her lips as she struggled to focus on him. Orient herself to her surroundings.

"What happened?"

"I was hoping you could tell me."

She closed her eyes again, her breathing coming more evenly. Was she fading away into unconsciousness again?

Then came a soft giggle.

She must be delirious. "Delaney?"

Her eyes opened again and a smile broadened. Then raising her other hand, she held out what appeared to be a five-inch piece of blue ribbon clenched between her fingers. "Got it."

She wasn't making any sense.

She pointed a finger upward, toward the top of the spindled staircase. "Someone missed the painter's tape. You'd already put the ladder away. But I got it. See?"

Triumphantly she waved the blue strip in his face.

He didn't know whether to shake her until her teeth rattled or pull her into his arms and never let her go.

But now wasn't a good time for either option. With the sound of an approaching siren, he knew the paramedics would be walking in any second.

Delaney struggled to sit up, but he placed a firm hand on her shoulder. "Hang on. Let's let these medical folks check you out. You could have a concussion or something."

And if she did, he'd take her back to Hunter's Hideaway for however long it took for her to recover. He could—

"If she's okay to travel, I'll take her back to Canyon Springs tonight."

Startled at the sound of a feminine voice, Luke turned to see Delaney's friend Paris standing just inside the door where Travis was waving down the paramedics. What was she doing here?

"I left my jacket on the fence," she said in response to his questioning look, "and had to come back to get it."

He turned again to Delaney, her eyes closed once more. He had so much to say to her. "Delaney, I—"

And then the emergency medical team came through the door. Luke stood and reluctantly moved away.

"So you see, Paris, there isn't anything to tell."

Following a brunch at Camilla's Café, Delaney and her friend hurried across the main thoroughfare in Canyon Springs the next morning. She might be more tired than usual, but otherwise none the worse for wear, although the slight knot on the back of her head remained tender.

"I know what I saw and what I heard." Paris's tone was adamant. "And it flies in the face of everything you're telling me."

"I'm sure I scared him, that's all. Nothing more. My laying there unconscious for those few minutes probably brought back bad memories. He's the one who found his wife after she'd—you know…"

"That could account for some of it, but not the look in his eyes. Believe me, I know love when I see it."

Delaney paused outside Dix's Woodland Warehouse, the ache in her heart not easing. "You know, Paris, this line of conversation isn't making me feel any better. I can only go by what Luke tells me. What he's decided. And that's that he cares for me. He doesn't deny it. But he doesn't love me enough to see another wife in his future. Door firmly closed."

"Somebody needs to knock some sense into him. Maybe I need to recruit Cody for a man-to-man intervention."

"Don't you dare." Having her friend's new husband stick his nose into it could only spell disaster.

"I'm frustrated. Here you are, two great people who have a once-in-a-lifetime opportunity to make each other happy and he's letting himself get stuck in the past."

"Healing takes time. He has a family to consider, too. A lot of responsibilities."

"Then why not lighten the burden with someone he loves? I don't get this at all."

Delaney didn't, either. Not really, although she'd thought and prayed about it continuously, trying to understand, to accept. She recognized that while God was sovereign, He didn't make people do things they didn't want to do. He gave them the gift of choice. And sometimes people made poor ones.

"So you're going to pack up and leave Hunter Ridge? No chance even for a long-distance romance?"

"I don't want a long-distance romance, Paris. I don't want a man who isn't capable of truly loving me—or letting me love him."

Paris sighed. "That's the kicker, isn't it? That he won't let you love him the way he needs to be loved."

"Exactly."

"When are you going back to Sacramento?"

"My doctor gave me a clean bill of health this morning, so I'm packing tomorrow. Pastor McCrae's arranged to have the furniture I borrowed from Aunt Jen and others returned to Canyon Springs after I've gone. I'll spend one last night at my cute Hunter Ridge place, then head out the next morning."

Why was she doing that? Why not come back to Canyon Springs and spend that final evening with family and friends? Why a last lonely night in Luke's hometown?

Because, try as she might to accept God's will, she didn't want to give Luke up.

Chapter Nineteen

"She'll think I've lost my mind, Chiffon." Luke murmured the words under his breath as he finished hitching the dapple gray mare to the surrey, his hands uncharacteristically unsteady as he secured the buckles. He hadn't harnessed a horse since he was a teen, but hopefully he'd gotten everything right. He gave the horse an affectionate pat, then cautiously led her to the open door of the stable where he paused to scan the property for meddlesome family members.

The coast was clear.

They moved forward into the late-afternoon sunshine, Chiffon stepping out alongside him as though knowing she had an important role to play. He adjusted the bit, the long length of reins, then climbed into the surrey and settled himself in. Hopefully driving a horse after so many years would be like riding a bike. He clucked to the mare and she moved forward.

Appearing out of nowhere to trot along beside them, Rags looked up hopefully and Luke halted the mare.

"You think you have to come along, too, I suppose." He patted the seat next to him. "Well, get up here, then."

The dog leaped into the surrey and sat down at his master's feet. Luke had just urged the horse forward when a familiar SUV drove up. He groaned as it angled to a stop in front of him and the driver's-side window rolled down.

Garrett. What was he doing here with that big smile plastered on his face?

"Taking Chiffon out for a little exercise, are you, Luke?" His cousin eyed the surrey with interest, no doubt noting the white shirt and Western hat, too. "If you're intending to exercise her all the way to town, you may want to make haste."

"Why's that?"

Garrett shrugged. "I just finished helping a certain woman load up her car."

Luke's heart jerked. "She's leaving? Today? I thought—"

"Why stick around for another night?" Garrett's exasperated glare more than made his point. "Nobody to my knowledge has given her any reason to."

"But she hasn't left yet?"

Garrett glanced at his watch. "Not as of about ten minutes ago."

He'd make better time in his pickup, wouldn't he? But how romantic was a pickup?

He pointed a commanding finger at Garrett.

"Don't go blabbing this all over the Hideaway, cuz. You hear me?"

"Lips are zipped, Romeo."

With a final warning glance in Garrett's direction, his heart pounding with a sense of urgency, Luke guided the mare around the SUV. Then trotted her down the graveled lane that led to the road to town. It was only a mile and a half. Maybe two.

God willing, he'd make it.

"Yes, I'll be back for Thanksgiving, Aunt Jen." How thankful she was that her aunt's chronic fatigue had turned out to be nothing more serious than an infected tooth that antibiotics and a root canal would soon remedy. "I wouldn't miss it for the world. Christmas, too."

Delaney sat on the front steps of her beloved summer property, her cell phone held to her ear. Yes, she'd come back to the Arizona high country. But would she ever be able to return without an ache in her heart? A shadow in her soul?

When the conversation wrapped up, she checked the time. There wasn't much point in hanging out here any longer. The original plan had been to stay one last night. But why? To provide God one more opportunity to give Luke a push?

"Give it up, girl." She rose from the steps and returned inside for one last look around, making sure she hadn't forgotten anything. As tempting as it was to deliberately forget something, hoping

Luke would contact her to arrange for its return, that would be manipulation. Not trusting God that He was in control.

Prolonging the pain.

Maybe she'd go as far as Flagstaff tonight, then hit I-40 west again in the morning.

At last she pulled the door shut and turned the key in the dead bolt. She'd told Garrett she'd drop off the key at the church office on her way out of town and he could return it for her.

Standing at the open car door, she gazed down the tree-lined main road winding through town, breathing in the scent of sun-warmed pine. Had it been two months since Luke had walked her through the property and handed her the keys? It seemed like only yesterday. Yet it felt like a thousand years since she'd last spoken to him.

"I guess this is it, Lord."

She slipped behind the steering wheel, pulled the door shut and started up the engine. Then with only a moment's hesitation, she put the car in Reverse and backed out.

I'm too late.

Her car was gone.

Luke clenched the reins in his hands as the surrey rounded a curve, his eyes scanning the length of the street ahead. Sometimes on a busy day, when the sandwich and pottery shops were humming, Delaney had to park farther from her place.

But there was no sign of the little red car.

His throat constricted as Chiffon's shod hooves on the hardtop surface echoed the aching knell tolling in his heart.

Why, God?

Unwilling to give up hope, he continued down the street where he guided the horse to pull up in front of Delaney's summer home. Maybe, just maybe…

But before he could step out of the surrey Sheree Aranda, owner of the Sandwich Emporium, came to the door of her shop, eyeing him curiously.

"If you're looking for Delaney, I saw her leave about twenty minutes ago. You might try calling her. She can't have gone too far."

A knot twisted in Luke's gut. A flash of anger. God had closed the door. Dare he defy that decision, call Delaney and attempt to pry it open? Climb through a window?

"I was stopping by to…so Chiffon here could say goodbye."

But from the sympathy darkening Sheree's eyes, he knew she wasn't buying a word of what he'd said. He tipped his Western hat in thanks. Then, checking to make sure traffic was clear, he tugged gently on the reins, signaling the mare to make a U-turn in the road. To head back home.

Without Delaney.

God had made a decision. Or had He? Hadn't

he himself played a part in the outcome of this as well? For so long he'd been unwilling to listen. Unwilling to allow his Heavenly Father to bear the burden of guilt he'd too-long carried. Unwilling to accept that God had a good plan for him. He'd rejected the very answer to his secret prayers for a life partner because he was too stubborn to recognize it. To recognize *her*.

Feeling curious eyes on him from every storefront he passed, he knew he should feel embarrassed. Humiliated at making a public spectacle of himself with a too-little-too-late effort. But there was no room in his heart for anything but the raw aching. The regret.

But not regret for having known Delaney.

Deep in thought, he leaned over to give Rags a pat. No, he might forever regret his own stupidity, but he'd never regret having had Delaney in his life, even for such a brief time. She and his kids had been the one bright spot in his life since Marsha passed away. She'd helped him get back on his feet. To trust God again. To reconnect with his dad and not compound the problem by running away to Kansas. Without question, he and his kids would live better lives having known her.

So how could he not trust God now? Not trust that everything worked for the good for those who loved God—even if it meant he'd never see Delaney again? Hadn't she told him when they first met that not everyone is meant to be in your life forever? Maybe she was a gift God had sent at a point in time when he needed her most. To serve a purpose.

Not for keeps.

His chest tightened at that recognition. But above all, he wanted God's will for his life and that of his children. What was best for Delaney.

Maybe God knows she's better off without me.

At his feet, Rags whined. Ears perked and moving his front paws restlessly, he focused on something farther down the street. He must see a squirrel. Or a cat. But before Luke could make a grab for his collar, Rags launched himself off the surrey.

"Hey! Get back here!"

Usually obedient, the dog paid him no mind, dashing to the edge of the walkway and weaving among startled pedestrians as he headed off to catch whatever had riveted his attention.

Great. Luke clucked to the mare to pick up her pace, his own gaze tracking the dog's erratic route.

And that's when, up ahead, he saw her.

Delaney.

Standing on the front steps of the Hunter Ridge Artists' Co-op, she was talking to Sunshine when Rags bounded up, tail wagging. With a smile of delight, she knelt to pet him as Sunshine returned inside.

His heart in his throat and the horse's hooves sounding loudly in his ears, Luke guided the surrey ever closer. Delaney gave Rags a final pat, then rose again to her feet. So beautiful in a faded denim sundress, golden waves of hair cascading over her shoulders, she lifted a hand to shield her eyes from the sun as her anxious gaze swept her surroundings.

As if looking for something. *Or someone?*

Stunned, Delaney stood all but openmouthed as Luke—handsome as any prince of her childhood dreams in black jeans and a white Western-cut shirt—approached in a surrey pulled by the gentle-natured Chiffon.

He tipped his hat, his gaze locked with hers.

Heart racing erratically, she watched as he drew the mare to a halt in front of the Co-op, secured the reins, then stepped out of the rig.

Aware that smiling shoppers had paused to take it all in, she gave a nervous laugh as Luke moved to Chiffon's head to adjust the bridle. Gently pushed away her inquiring nose. Then he placed his hands on his hips in that oh-so-familiar stance. "Where are you parked?"

Hope plummeted. He was here to give her a ride to her car? She'd read too much into what she'd unwisely assumed was a romantic gesture. Silly her. Of course he'd want to say goodbye. To ensure that things between them ended on a good note. "Around back. There wasn't any place close by on the street and I just wanted to see Sunshine for a few minutes."

He nodded, then stepped to the side of the surrey, his hand outstretched in invitation. His expression unreadable. "Would you care to join me?"

For a lifetime. But this was goodbye. "I'd love to."

Taking her hand, he helped her into the surrey and Rags leaped up into the seat behind her. She self-consciously straightened her skirt as Luke, with a tight smile and a tip of his hat to the curious onlookers, moved around to the other side to climb in. Then without a word, he slapped the reins lightly and Chiffon moved forward, her ears flicking back and forth as the clip-clop, clip-clop of her hooves echoed a soothing rhythm.

They rode along in silence for what seemed like an eternity, Delaney's hands clasped in her lap, but her mind racing. Dreading what was yet to come. She didn't want to hear again why it wasn't in God's plans for them to have a future together. She could only pray that he'd get whatever he intended to say over with quickly. But he hadn't turned down the alley leading to the parking lot in back of the Co-op, so where was he taking her?

"Pretty dress," he said at long last. But he didn't look at her.

She took a slow breath. "Thank you. I bought it here in town. It's hand embroidered."

He nodded. Flicked the reins.

"Nice shirt," she reciprocated after a too-long silence and he turned to look at her, an unexpected spark of amusement in his eyes.

"Thanks." He clucked to the mare, guiding her off the main road to the pine-lined lane leading to Hunter's Hideaway.

She took a deep breath, garnering her courage. There was no point in dragging this out. She didn't want to go to the Hideaway. Didn't want to hear whatever was on Luke's mind. She just wanted to get in her car and go. "You know, Luke, I'm not into long goodbyes…"

He stared ahead, as if finding something fascinating on the tips of Chiffon's ears. "Does this have to be goodbye?"

What was he saying? That he wanted to stay in touch? Be friends?

"I don't understand."

Gravel crunched under the surrey's wheels as the sun slanted down through the ponderosa branches. Birds twittered.

They rode along for several more minutes. Was he not going to explain himself? But just as she was frustrated enough to leap from the moving carriage and walk back to town, he guided the mare off the lane and into a stand of pines. Drew her to a halt.

He secured the reins, his gaze solemn. "I'm sorry, Delaney."

What was he apologizing for?

"I'm sorry—" he reached for her hand and took it in his "—if I ever gave you the impression that I considered you just one of the kids."

She didn't want to hear this, and tried to pull her hand away, but he held on tight.

"I never saw you like that, Delaney. Never. But telling myself that, well, it let me lie to myself. Lie that you weren't coming to mean so much to me."

They'd already been over this ground. Yes, he *cared* for her. But he didn't love her. Not the way you loved someone you wanted to share your life with. Like she loved him. "Luke—"

He tugged gently on her hand, his gaze now intent. "Listen to me, Delaney. Please? I'm doing my best not to be controlling here, but given that you're in such an all-fired hurry to get out of town—" He reached for her other hand, held both of them gently in his, his gaze now locked on hers. "I love you, Delaney. Will you marry me?"

She gasped.

"Sorry about the ambush." He offered a lopsided smile. "But you gave me no choice."

She stared at him. Had she heard right? He wanted to *marry* her? "But I thought… I don't understand. What's changed, Luke?"

"Me." He linked his fingers with hers. "When you knocked yourself unconscious, when I was afraid I'd lose you, I finally got it through my thick head that there are many things that are out of our control. That life is too short and unpredictable not to accept the good gifts God offers us. And that…" He looked down at their intertwined fingers, then back into her eyes. "And that I don't want to live my life without you in it."

Was she dreaming?

But dreaming or not, she pulled her hands free to throw her arms around his neck.

Laughing, he gathered her into his arms. Strong arms. So secure. So right. "So that's a yes, Delaney?"

She pulled back slightly to look into his smiling eyes. "Yes, yes, yes. Oh, my goodness, yes!"

He laughed again as he brushed back the hair from her face. "I love you, Delaney. I mean that. You've brightened my world in more ways than I can count, and I can only pray that I can give back to you even half of what you've given me."

"You've more than done that already." She drew back to look at him. "I love you, too, Luke. My own superhero."

He chuckled. "I don't know about *that*."

"I do."

"Say that again." He cupped his ear as if listening intently. "I want you to have those exact two words memorized for a walk down the aisle."

Her heart swelled with joy. "We're really getting married, Luke?"

He slipped his arm around her waist. "The sooner the better, as far as I'm concerned."

She nodded, still not quite sure she wasn't

dreaming. "Nothing big that takes a lot of time to plan."

"That works for me." Luke cocked his head. "Maybe we can get Garrett to conduct a drive-thru next weekend?"

Laughing, she poked him lightly in the chest. "Don't push it, superhero."

He tightened his grip around her. Pulled her close. "A guy in love has to try."

He loved her. Wanted to *marry* her. Make her his wife. The mother to his three precious children.

Suddenly, eyes wide, she pulled back and gripped his arm. "Luke! The kids! What will your kids think?"

Smiling, he cupped her face in his hand. "*Our* kids. And our kids—present and future—will think this is the best decision we've ever made."

"You're okay with more kids?" She gazed uncertainly into his eyes. "I wasn't sure…you know, with you already having three."

"We can have as many as you can handle, Delaney. So be careful what you wish for."

She gave him a hug. "I love you, Luke Hunter."

"And I love you, Delaney Marks."

She drew back again. "What do you think? Should we go tell *our* kids the happy news?"

"I'm all for that. But first…" Eyes twinkling, he looked around them as if confirming they were alone. His arms tightened around her as he leaned in close. "How about a kiss, pretty lady?"

Epilogue

"Congratulations, Mom and Dad!"

Gazing into the smiling faces of Chloe, Anna and Travis, tears dampened Delaney's eyes as she and Luke—Mr. and Mrs. Luke Hunter—stepped arm in arm from the church sanctuary and into the bright September sun. A beautiful Saturday morning on Labor Day weekend.

A rousing cheer went up from their friends and family.

With the help of Paris and Aunt Jen, they had managed to pull together an unforgettable wedding on short notice. It had been perfect in every way, leaving her no doubt that the reception at Hunter's Hideaway would be every bit as beautiful.

Luke—her husband—leaned down to give her his handkerchief and she gently dabbed it at her eyes. Thank goodness for waterproof mascara. "I'm going to look like a bawl-baby in all our photographs."

"A beautiful bawl-baby." He gave her a quick kiss.

"Come on, Dad. Plenty of time for the mushy

stuff later. Food awaits." Travis impulsively slipped his arm around his father for a warm embrace.

"I'm beautiful, too." Chloe spun around in her bridesmaid dress, arms raised like a ballerina.

"Yes, you are." Luke nodded to Anna, as well. "You, too, sweetheart."

Travis's lower lip protruded as he thrust his thumbs under the lapels of his tux. "What about me?"

Delaney laughed. "You're beautifully handsome, Trav. And I think from the look in Scottie's eyes, she would agree."

"Yeah?" He looked around in search of his girlfriend. "You guys don't plan to hang out here much longer, do you? I'm starving." He grasped his jaw. "I think all those photos wore out my smile, too."

"Think of the brunch that awaits you," Delaney reminded. "I imagine that will revive it."

As Travis took off, Luke motioned to an approaching Garrett and Grady. "You two cleaned up pretty good, didn't you? Made Grandma Jo proud. Now if you can find a woman who'll put up with you long enough to wrestle a ring onto her finger, you're both good to go."

Grady elbowed Garrett. "Look who's suddenly the relationship expert."

"Yeah, but he can't claim any credit for it."

Garrett gave Delaney a conspiratorial grin. "He has this lady to thank."

Delaney happily looped her arm through Luke's and smiled up at him. "I admit he may be a slow learner but, once he caught on, he's making up for it."

Luke cocked an arrogant brow at his brother and cousin. "Hear that, boys?"

"Yeah, yeah." Grady good-naturedly waved him off, then lifted Chloe into his arms and turned to Anna. "What do you say, ladies, if we head out to the Hideaway and make sure the party's rolling by the time your mom and dad get there?"

Mom and Dad.

A happy shiver danced up Delaney's spine at those words. She hadn't been sure what Luke's children would want to call her and had assumed it would be Delaney since that's the name they'd always called her. But last night, after the rehearsal dinner, the three of them pulled her and Luke aside, announcing their unanimous decision.

Mom.

As Garrett, Grady and the girls headed to the parking lot, Delaney and Luke continued to receive handshakes and hugs of congratulations from family and friends hailing from both Canyon Springs and Hunter Ridge. Only three months ago she'd never have imagined she'd be standing here today as the *wife* of Luke Hunter.

"You're lost in thought, pretty lady." Luke

slipped his arm around her and, still smiling, leaned in close as at last they arrived at Luke's gaily decorated pickup truck, a sign on the tailgate declaring JUST MARRIED. "What are you thinking about? How handsome I am?"

"Without a doubt. But also…" She wasn't quite sure how to put her thoughts, her feelings, into words. "I feel…"

So much. So many different things. Joy. Awe. Anticipation. Thankfulness.

"I feel for the first time since I lost my family to that accident…that I've truly come home."

She again blinked back tears, too overcome to speak as he gathered her into the security of his arms.

"I feel the same, as if returning from a too-long-journey." His eyes smiled into hers. "My heart will forever belong to you, my beautiful Delaney. Welcome home to us both."

* * * * *

Dear Reader,

Have you ever noticed that dwelling excessively on the past—or on the worst that could happen in the future—steals enjoyment from the present?

That's the situation in which Delaney Marks and Luke Hunter find themselves—and it's keeping them apart. Both have suffered great tragedies. Luke allows the past not only to dictate his future but to drive him to try to control it. And Delaney allows the fear of losing those she loves to lead her to expect and brace herself for inevitable loss. Both must come to trust that God is in control, that He heals past wounds and holds the future, freeing them to live in the present with joy.

As with my series set in fictional Canyon Springs, Arizona, nearby Hunter Ridge is nestled in the rugged ponderosa pine mountain country. The stories set here will explore the lives and loves of men and women who have always called this place home, who once fled its city limits and are now returning, or who are stepping into the little community for the very first time. Join them on their journey to love and becoming all God wants them to be. Welcome to Hunter Ridge!

You can contact me via email at glynna@glynnakaye.com or Love Inspired Books, 233 Broadway, Suite 1001, New York, NY 10279. Please visit my website at glynnakaye.com—and stop by loveinspiredauthors.com, seekerville.net, and seekerville.blogspot.com.

Glynna Kaye

LARGER-PRINT BOOKS!

GET 2 FREE
LARGER-PRINT NOVELS
PLUS 2 FREE
MYSTERY GIFTS

Love Inspired®

Larger-print novels are now available...

LARGER-PRINT BOOKS!

GET 2 FREE LARGER-PRINT NOVELS PLUS 2 FREE MYSTERY GIFTS

Love Inspired®

SUSPENSE

RIVETING INSPIRATIONAL ROMANCE

Larger-print novels are now available...

YES! Please send me 2 FREE LARGER-PRINT Love Inspired® Suspense novels and my 2 FREE mystery gifts (gifts are worth about $10). After receiving them, if I don't wish to receive any more books, I can return the shipping statement marked "cancel." If I don't cancel, I will receive 4 brand-new novels every month and be billed just $5.49 per book in the U.S. or $5.99 per book in Canada. That's a savings of at least 19% off the cover price. It's quite a bargain! Shipping and handling is just 50¢ per book in the U.S. and 75¢ per book in Canada.* I understand that accepting the 2 free books and gifts places me under no obligation to buy anything. I can always return a shipment and cancel at any time. Even if I never buy another book, the two free books and gifts are mine to keep forever.

110/310 IDN GH6P

Name	(PLEASE PRINT)	
Address		Apt. #
City	State/Prov.	Zip/Postal Code

Signature (if under 18, a parent or guardian must sign)

Mail to the Reader Service:
IN U.S.A.: P.O. Box 1867, Buffalo, NY 14240-1867
IN CANADA: P.O. Box 609, Fort Erie, Ontario L2A 5X3

Are you a current subscriber to Love Inspired® Suspense books and want to receive the larger-print edition?
Call 1-800-873-8635 or visit www.ReaderService.com.

* Terms and prices subject to change without notice. Prices do not include applicable taxes. Sales tax applicable in N.Y. Canadian residents will be charged applicable taxes. Offer not valid in Quebec. This offer is limited to one order per household. Not valid for current subscribers to Love Inspired Suspense larger-print books. All orders subject to credit approval. Credit or debit balances in a customer's account(s) may be offset by any other outstanding balance owed by or to the customer. Please allow 4 to 6 weeks for delivery. Offer available while quantities last.

Your Privacy—The Reader Service is committed to protecting your privacy. Our Privacy Policy is available online at www.ReaderService.com or upon request from the Reader Service.

We make a portion of our mailing list available to reputable third parties that offer products we believe may interest you. If you prefer that we not exchange your name with third parties, or if you wish to clarify or modify your communication preferences, please visit us at www.ReaderService.com/consumerchoice or write to us at Reader Service Preference Service, P.O. Box 9062, Buffalo, NY 14240-9062. Include your complete name and address.

LISLP15